Also by Jan Springer

A Hero Escapes
A Hero Betrayed
A Hero's Kiss
A Hero Wanted
Captive Heroes

Pleasure Bound Boxed Set
Pleasure Bound : COMPLETE SERIES SciFi Erotic Romance Boxed Set

Tentacles Shifter Erotic Romance
Taken by Him

The Key Club
A Merry Menage Christmas
Sophie's Menage
Jewel's Menage
Jaxie's Menage
A Homecoming Menage Christmas

The Outlaw Lovers
Jude
The Claiming
Colter's Revenge
Tyler's Woman
Resistance

The Outlaw Lovers
Alpha Outlaws Boxed Set

Vampira
Sweet Heat
Wet Heat
Crimson Heat

Standalone
A Touch of Menage Boxed Set
Shades of Menage Boxed Set
Naughty Girl Desires Boxed Set
Nice Girl Naughty
Sinderella Sexy
The Biker and The Bride
The Fire Within
Bared to Him
Pleasure Bound : A Futuristic Adult Romance Boxed Set
Merry Menage Kisses Boxed Set
Stripped Naked
Risqué Girl Delights Boxed Set
A Holiday Menage
Ménage À Trois
A Hitman for Hannah
Billionaire Boyfriend

Watch for more at www.janspringer.com.

Jade's Fantasy
Kidnap Fantasies 1
Jan Springer

In the land of the rich and famous, Kidnap Fantasies is the answer to discreet naughty downtime.

When ex-downhill skier Jade's two sisters give her a Kidnap Fantasies questionnaire, Jade is aroused at the prospect of having no-strings fun in the sun with a stranger whose only job would be to fulfill her every intimate fantasy. Although she knows she's too shy to send it in, she secretly pours her deepest wishes into the questionnaire.

Soon the questionnaire mysteriously vanishes and Jade's fantasy man appears on her luxury yacht in the form of a sexy handy man who gives her an intimate toy-filled Christmas holiday she'll never forget.

Jade's Fantasy

Published by Spunky Girl Publishing
Copyright 2015 Jan Springer
2nd edition
Cover Art by Talina Perkins of Bookin' It Designs
Edited by Amelia S. Black

License Notes

Chapter One

Tampa Bay, Florida USA
Four days before Christmas...

"It's really called Kidnap Fantasies?" Jade asked her two sisters, as she poured each of them another glass of iced tea, and sliced some more strawberry cheesecake.

"That's what it's called," Jillian said. "Kidnap Fantasies."

Jillian and Johnna had flown into town unexpectedly yesterday to give her the fascinating news that Johnna was about one month pregnant and Jade and Jillian would become aunts in the summer.

The baby would be their first niece or nephew and Jade was ecstatic.

Yesterday the three of them had gone on a shopping spree for baby stuff and Christmas presents until they'd dropped from exhaustion and then watched movies into the wee hours last night just like when they'd been teenagers. Now they sat at the table on the upper deck of Jade's yacht discussing Jillian's idea of indulging in some sort of sexual tryst with a stranger through Kidnap Fantasies.

In a matter of minutes, they would be leaving to go home and Jade wanted to get the scoop about this Kidnap Fantasies, before they left.

"How'd you hear about it?" Jade prodded.

An odd gleam sparkled Jillian's blue eyes. "From an acquaintance."

"You're seriously considering hiring a strange man to have sex with you?"

"Why not? Isn't it every woman's fantasy to be swept off her feet by a completely gorgeous stranger and have her deepest sexual desires fulfilled by him over and over again?"

"I know I was swept off my feet by my stranger." Johnna chimed in.

"You mean by Jeff's hunky body and all those nice muscles," Jillian chuckled.

"A man only needs one very well working muscle to satisfy a woman." Johnna leaned back in the deck chair. Her shoulder-length brown hair fluttered in the Florida breeze. She inhaled and smiled dreamily. "And his big muscle most certainly does the job quite well."

Oh my God! Her sisters were at it again—talking about sex.

Her face warmed with embarrassment. She'd never been particularly comfortable talking about the subject but this sex group had piqued her interest and was forcing her to overcome her shyness.

"But to have yourself kidnapped? I mean what if he..."

What if he did all the naughty things you've always dreamed of, a little voice purred in her ear.

"Don't look so shocked, sweetie." Jillian laughed, "Some women love to be sexually dominated in the bedroom."

"Yeah, but is it legal?"

"What? Being dominated in the bedroom?" Jillian winked at Johnna. Both sisters seemed to be trying to keep a straight face. Obviously, they still enjoyed teasing her about sex. Some things never changed.

She exhaled in frustration. "C'mon, I mean Kidnap Fantasies."

"Oh! Well, let's just say they prefer not to advertise to the public. Only a select group of the rich and famous knows about it." Jillian picked up last week's edition of People magazine with the recent picture of Jade holding her newly released autobiography about her life as a professional downhill skier. "And you're famous, sis. So I've just let you in on the secret club, but you can't tell anyone about this organization."

Jade's excitement plunged. "So it isn't legal."

"How can something be illegal if it doesn't exist?" Johnna winked.

"You sound intrigued, and a little nervous." Jillian leaned forward, her face suddenly very serious. It made Jade a tad uneasy. "You wouldn't by any chance be interested in checking out this Kidnap Fantasies for yourself would you?" she asked.

"Oh no, I couldn't!" Jade said it so fast that both her sisters smiled knowingly.

"Nice reaction, Jade." Johnna chuckled, her ice blue eyes flashing with amusement. "Exactly how long has it been since you've been properly fucked by a man?"

Extreme heat flushed her cheeks giving her away at Johnna's bold question. Twenty-eight years old and her face still flamed with embarrassment over the subject of sex. She took a quick gulp of her cold drink but it did nothing to cool her uneasiness.

"That long, huh?" Jillian replied.

"It's not that I haven't wanted to...it's just since the accident."

Jillian winced. Her gaze quickly strayed to Jade's cane where she'd hung it earlier from the back of her lounge chair.

"The accident was a year ago. You said your therapists are happy with your progress and you sure are walking a heck of a lot better since the last time we saw you. So what's preventing you from going after a man?"

Jade shrugged, "My scars for one thing."

"Oh please, the scars on your leg are barely visible. Any guy would be thrilled to go out with you. You are beautiful, Jade," Jillian said in a reassuring voice.

"I've packed on twenty pounds..."

"Cut the crap," Johnna interjected. "You were too skinny before. Tell me this, does your hesitation have something to do with Beau?" The earlier amusement had disappeared from Johnna's voice replaced by one of contempt as she spoke about Jade's ex-fiancé.

Again, Jade shrugged.

"You're better off without that creep," Johnna continued. "Besides not all men are like that. Look at Jeff. He's absolutely adorable. You said so yourself."

That was true. Johnna and Jeff were so much in love. Jade had met him a couple of times before their June wedding and she couldn't help but wish for a sexy blue-eyed guy like Jeff for her very own. Husky body. Lots of nice muscles. And the love that shone in his eyes for her sister had taken Jade's breath away. She'd do anything to have a guy look at her the way Jeff looked at Johnna but it didn't mean she had to trust one again.

"I'm not ready for a relationship," she admitted.

"Okay, so what you're saying is you're ready for some good old-fashioned sex without the strings of a relationship. Kidnap Fantasies is perfect for you. Here..." Jillian slid a thick brochure across the table at Jade. "It sounds like you're the one who needs Kidnap Fantasies more than I do. Take a look at it. It is their latest catalogue and there's even a questionnaire in there. Why don't you fill it out tonight for fun?"

Jade slipped on her reading glasses and slid her fingers across the velvety softness of the brochure with the dark blue cover and sharp pink lettering. She tried hard to resist the urge to start flipping through the catalogue right then, and there.

The idea of having sex with a complete stranger without strings attached made her pulse race with excitement. She'd had fantasies about how a man would use sex toys on her and tease her until she screamed for mercy but she'd never actually had the nerve to walk into one of those shops and get a toy or ask her ex-fiancé Beau if he might want to explore that angle in their stagnant sex life.

He'd been a missionary man.

Slam. Bam. Thank you, ma'am.

This Kidnap Fantasies just might be a nice way to live out some of her fantasies. The best thing was she wouldn't have to be embarrassed because she'd never see the guy again.

"These men...who do this type of thing," Jade asked. "Are they safe?"

"I believe you're talking of STDs and stuff. The men and women are screened with great care. From what I've learned the participants are rich and famous themselves and are looking for a little casual sex in between relationships but don't want any media attention or paparazzi around so they go to KF. Everything is confidential. It's a tight little group. Call it a club. Everyone knows everyone. Besides, KF, wouldn't be in business long if they didn't make sure their people were safe and happy, right? It's all there in the brochure." Jillian glanced at her watch and frowned. "Well, it's time to meet our flights, Johnna. We're both going to have to get a move on."

"Can't you guys stay an extra night? Just this once? I miss you both so much."

"Sorry Jade, I promised Jeff I'd only be a couple of days and that I'd be back in time to do some serious last-minute Christmas shopping with him." Johnna replied.

"And I've got important meetings scheduled all the way through to Christmas Eve that I can't cancel," Jillian said quickly hugging her so tightly she thought they'd squeeze her to death.

"Merry Christmas, Jade." Jillian whispered into her ear.

"And you take care of yourself, sis. Merry Christmas, sweetie," Johnna said as she kissed Jade on the cheek.

"Thanks for all the Christmas presents, you guys," Jade replied as she hugged them back. "And Johnna, take care of yourself. No stress. It's not good for the baby."

When they let go of her, she didn't miss the tears sparkling in both her sisters' eyes. Before she could question why they suddenly looked so...conflicted, both were waving to her and heading down the stairs to the main deck.

If she could walk as fast as they could, she would have sprinted after them and asked what was going on but right now, she was useless. Her hip had stiffened up as it always did from sitting for too long in one stretch.

The familiar shard of sadness tugged at her emotions as she watched her two sisters wave yet again and then they disappeared behind another docked boat.

Her sisters were so lucky. Both were confident women. Knew what they wanted and went after it. Not like her. Her whole life had been her passion for skiing. That was gone now thanks to her accident. All she had left was lots of money, a crippled body and no man to love her or call her own...not that she wanted one...but it would have been nice if men weren't such no-good louses and so untrustworthy.

Her sadness quickly disintegrated as she settled her attention to the snappy-looking Kidnap Fantasies brochure Jillian had left behind.

Too bad she had a get-together with her agent this afternoon. The woman was trying to talk Jade into agreeing to a meeting with a prominent talk show host who wanted her on his show to talk about her autobiography.

If Jade agreed to the appearance, it would get her book more exposure. Exposure she really didn't want.

However, hindsight was twenty-twenty. It had been a silly thing to write her life story. She knew it now but after her accident, she'd needed something to do besides feeling sorry for herself. Writing the book had helped her a lot. Unfortunately, since the book had released, the paparazzi had been coming out of the woodwork back in Los Angeles. She'd even found one of them sitting on top of the security wall surrounding her home. He'd had a camera with the longest zoom lens she'd ever seen. To her embarrassment, he'd been taking pictures of her sunbathing topless.

The next day her picture had been plastered over all the gossip rags. That had been the last straw. She'd packed up her bags, dressed incognito and taken refuge here under the warm Tampa Bay sun in her yacht just in time for her sisters' surprise meeting.

Boy was she ever glad they'd mentioned Kidnap Fantasies. Throwing a longing look at the catalog, she placed it inside a nearby locker, grabbed her cane and hobbled toward her bedroom just inside the glass door. Barely able to contain the tingles of excitement and the cheerful giggles at the thought that she was actually thinking she might hire a man to satisfy her sexual fantasies, Jade reluctantly got ready for her appointment with her agent.

* * * * *

It wasn't until late that night when Jade had snuggled herself into her cozy king-sized bed in her yacht bedroom, thrown a light sheet over her nude body, propped herself up on an elbow and slipped on her glasses that she dare examine the Kidnap Fantasies brochure Jillian had given her.

The minute she flipped it open her mouth dropped in surprise at the words splashed across the first page.

Ménage a Trois. BDSM. Sex Slave Training. Kidnap Fantasies. Whatever your sexual wish we'll fill your desires. Complete the questionnaire and let our discreet Kidnap Fantasies liaisons set you free.

Sweet heavens! What had she gotten herself into?

Well, she hadn't gotten into anything yet but by the delicious way her pussy muscles were clenching with excitement Jade knew she already liked what she saw.

As she turned the pages and read the vivid descriptions, her heart picked up speed and she slipped a hand over one of her breasts. She plucked and toyed with her plump nipple wondering how it would feel to have a gorgeous man touching her breasts as she was doing now.

Beau hadn't really bothered priming her for sex. So, she had little experience being intimately touched by a man.

Would her nipples harden beneath a man's calloused fingers in the same way they were hardening now? Or would if feel different? Would her breasts swell with need as he gazed upon her nakedness, lust shining brightly in his eyes?

Jade inhaled an aroused breath. Her fantasy man's hands would be big enough to cup her breasts, his fingers long and thick enough to do some heavy duty massaging on her clit and then to slide deep inside her vagina so he could finger-fuck her.

Her pussy moistened at that idea.

Wow! She definitely needed some woman to man, hot flesh-to-flesh contact.

Her gaze flicked back to the brochure. If she went with the Ménage á Trois Special, she'd have to give Kidnap Fantasies permission to have her kidnapped by two strange men who would sexually satisfy her for one glorious weekend. In the Sex Slave Fantasy, she could order herself to be kidnapped and trained in a dungeon as a sex slave for a month. Then there was an Emerald City fantasy. A woman would give the organization permission to allow herself to be whisked away to a fantasyland where she could experience multiple ménages with the Scarecrow, Tin Man, Cowardly Lion and the Wizard of Oz.

And there were other exciting options that left Jade breathless as she tried to decide which one she'd like to try.

What finally caught her eye was the kidnap fantasy with one man who would fulfill her every sexual wish for a weekend.

She'd fill out the questionnaire.

Grabbing a pen, she ripped the forms out of the brochure and began to answer the questions.

Name: Jade Hart.

Age: 28.

Sex: Female.

Sexual preference: Hot-blooded Male.

Sexual experience?

Jade laughed and wrote—not much...actually only one man. Missionary style. Vanilla sex. Boring.

She continued down the list answering more questions and then hesitated at one in particular—How well-hung do you want your man to be?

She inhaled softly at that question. Dropping her pen, she flopped onto her back, closed her eyes and began a slow massage on her nipples. She relished the idea of how big her dream man would be and how he'd fill the lovely ache beginning to erupt between her thighs.

Beau's cock had been on the small and short side never quite reaching the needy ache deep within, leaving her sexually hungry and craving for more.

What she wanted was a man who'd make her scream lustily like those heroines did at the hands of their well-endowed heroes in the erotic-romance electronic books she downloaded into her handy electronic book reader.

She kneaded her breasts harder inhaling at the wonderful way her nipples stiffened beneath her fingers.

What she craved was intense sexual satisfaction at a man's expert hands. What she wanted was a man's hard calloused fingers gliding over her breasts. A man with wide strong shoulders she could grab onto as he slid his thick, giant cock into her, stretching her open wide. A giant velvet rock-hard cock with pulsing veins that she could wrap her mouth around and suck and taste and just feel a man's power.

Jade's eyes snapped open. Her hands left her breasts. She rolled to her side and grabbed her pen again.

Very well-hung, she giggled as she continued to write. The bigger, the better.

Oh, don't be shy!

The biggest cock you've got in stock.

With each question, Jade's boldness grew and her arousal blossomed. Gosh, some of these questions sounded delicious while others turned her right off.

But that was the whole point, wasn't it? To give the well-hung man of her dreams a bird's-eye view of what she wanted.

Completing the questionnaire, Jade sighed wistfully.

Wouldn't it be something if she actually had the nerve to send the questionnaire to Kidnap Fantasies?

No, she couldn't do that. Having a strange man make love to her wasn't romantic. But she wasn't looking for romance. She just wanted to be fucked by a big strong man. Wanted to dull the ache between her legs. Wished for a man's long, thick cock to slide into her and claim her.

Jade bit her bottom lip thoughtfully.

Jillian did say the medical histories of those men were checked out. Wouldn't it be wild to have a well-hung, good-looking man fucking her senseless?

A man who would spread her legs far apart.

Jade pushed the sheets aside, lifted her knees and spread her legs wide, trying not to wince at the dull ache deep inside her injured hip.

He would be a man who would not be afraid to touch a woman where she needed to be touched.

She slid a hand between her thighs and slipped a finger between her puffed labia.

Gosh, her pussy felt as if it were on fire.

Actually, her entire body burned at the thought of a man standing right here in front of her. His muscles gleaming with perspiration, his massive cock stretching straight out in front of him, rigid and solid and wanting to fuck her so bad he could barely stand.

Jade smiled and teased her sensitive clit with torturous slow strokes.

She liked the thought of a man wanting her that bad. A man who couldn't keep his hands off her. A man who would feel comfortable enough for both of them to persuade her into experimenting with the fantasies she'd just written down on the questionnaire.

She slipped a finger inside her wet vagina and collected some moisture withdrawing and massaging her clitoris once again.

Her other hand settled back on her breast and she kneaded her sensitive pink nipple watching it elongate with arousal. She continued to massage her clit, tightening her abdominal muscles and then dipping inside her soaked vagina collecting more juices to then rub against her slippery pearl.

Her well-hung man would be honest. Trustworthy. Good-looking.

A man who liked to surprise her with presents and flowers and...sex toys.

Definitely sex toys.

She slipped her finger into her wet vagina. With her other hand, she continued to stroke her breasts and her stiff nipples.

Her breathing quickened.

She closed her eyes as the slow burn began to unravel.

Another finger slipped inside her slit and she slid in and out in quick experienced strokes. Her other hand flew away from her breast and she rubbed her clit in strong firm movements.

Her man would plunge his cock deep into her pussy in hard, pounding thrusts. His groans of arousal would rip through the air and join her whimpers of pleasure.

Jade smiled as she envisioned their two perspiration-drenched bodies writhing on her bed, the sharp sound of their bodies slamming into each other, the sexy scent of their passion seeping into her lungs.

Fire erupted deep in the pit of her belly and in a second, she was lost in the orgasm. She rode the pleasure waves that ripped through her belly.

Her nerve endings sizzled. Her mouth dropped open as she cried out her release.

Opening her eyes, she watched her legs tremble and her hips gyrate beneath the powerful orgasm as her hands moved masterfully between her legs. Her pink nipples stabbed into the air. Her breasts jiggled sensuously with her every breath.

Oh God! She needed a man to do this to her!

Too soon, the orgasm ebbed leaving Jade panting and alone on her bed.

She eyed the questionnaire sheets and frowned.

She'd poured her heart into that survey and yet it would never be seen by anyone other than herself because no matter how much she wanted to have a strange man doing delightful things to her body she knew she was just too chicken to mail it in.

Three days before Christmas...

"Hello! Jade, honey!" Jillian's voice echoed through the early morning ocean mist as she and Johnna stepped onto Jade's yacht.

No answer.

Jillian smiled and her heart pounded with excitement.

She and Johnna had watched from behind a nearby building as Jade ambled down the dock with her cane and gotten into a waiting limo.

"Where do you think she put it?" Johnna asked from behind her.

Knowing that Jade's bedroom was toward the end of her yacht, Jillian motioned Johnna to follow. A moment later, they were peeking into the bedroom windows.

Bingo. Jillian smiled when she spotted the Kidnap Fantasies brochure lying smack in the middle of the rumpled sheets of Jade's bed. Her hopes plummeted.

"I see the brochure, but no questionnaire."

"I see it," Johnna giggled. "Right over there on her night table. Do you really think she filled it out?"

"If I know our middle sister, she's fantasized and filled it out...however, mailing it would be the problem. And that's what the good Lord created sisters for. To keep an eye on her and help her out."

A moment later, Jillian was not surprised to discover Jade's bedroom door unlocked. Her sister had always been that way. Too trusting of everyone around her. That's why that no good fiancé of hers had so easily broken Jade's heart.

Well, it wouldn't happen this time. This time Jade would have Kidnap Fantasies at her back. The organization hadn't been in business and such a huge secret if they did things wrong.

"Do you think she'll realize it is missing?" Johnna asked as Jillian slipped the questionnaire into her purse.

The urge to read it was great but she valued her sister's privacy. Only a handful of people who would see the questionnaire, the owners of Kidnap Fantasies and the man they picked to give Jade her fantasies.

"Hopefully she'll think she misplaced it," Jillian replied as they quickly left the bedroom and headed off the yacht. "Besides, that hundred dollar bill that I slipped the security guard should take care of her having no clue we're still in town."

"Are you sure we have to be so sneaky, Jillian?" Guilt laced Johnna's voice.

"As I just said, we're being helpful. You saw the excitement and shyness on her face when we were talking about Kidnap Fantasies. She wants this. She's just too shy to do anything about it."

Jillian nodded and sighed with relief.

Thankfully, Johnna understood why it had to go this way. If everything went according to plan, their sister Jade would be experiencing some much-needed sex with no strings and hopefully a much needed boost to her confidence.

Chapter Two

Two days before Christmas...

Chestnuts roasting over an open fire, Jack Frost nipping at your nose...

The song blared from the nearest marina speaker set high on a pole right beside Jade's yacht.

Silly Christmas music! Why couldn't they shut it off, for crying out loud? With Christmas fast approaching most of the nearby yachts and the marina was practically deserted. Except for the jolly female security guard at the marina entrance, no one else seemed to be around for the holiday season.

So, who in the world were they playing these Christmas tunes for?

If she wasn't enjoying the heat from the warm sunshine washing over her skimpy thong and caressing her naked breasts she'd have given the marina guard a call by now and told her where to shove that racket!

Jade frowned.

She knew why she was in such a rotten mood. It was exactly one year ago today that Beau had become engaged to that other woman. The last thing she felt like doing today was listening to bright season's carols. Even yesterday's second round of meetings with her agent and then again this morning when she'd hit the shopping malls to hunt for more cute baby clothes for her upcoming niece or nephew she'd been bombarded with cheerful salespeople wishing her season's greetings.

Pooh! She just couldn't get away from Christmas.

She frowned and sipped on her tequila. The warm liquid almost made her gag. She hated warm drinks!

Plopping the snifter onto the nearby table, she grabbed the Kidnap Fantasies brochure and slid her glasses on trying her darnedest to tune out the music.

The words in the brochure grabbed her attention yet again and her heart picked up a quick pace as she read.

16

Sex slave training.

BDSM specials. Bondage. Kidnap fantasies.

Sexual adventures including being kidnapped and taken to a nudist colony, outdoor adventures such as being hunted down by a man in the woods, or having sex in public places or in front of other people.

If she hadn't misplaced that questionnaire she just might have gotten up the nerve to send it in. Last night her body had burned bright with fevered lust just thinking about a strange man fucking her senseless.

This afternoon when she'd come back from shopping, she'd been on the edge of mailing the questionnaire. Unfortunately, she couldn't remember where she'd put it. That just wouldn't do. It would be quite embarrassing if the housekeeper found it next week.

Jade would have to do a thorough search of her bedroom before that happened. But right now, she wanted to suck up some rays and just think about nothing.

The song on the marina speakers switched over to "I'll Be Home For Christmas". Sadness tugged at her heart. No one would be coming home for Christmas for her this year. No big deal, though. She'd get used to being alone through the holidays.

She'd done it last year.

Johnna had spent it trapped in a snowbound cabin with a sexy stranger who she was now married to and Jillian hadn't been able to get away to spend Christmas with her because the airports had been shut down due to bad weather.

Just the other day when Johnna had asked her if she'd like to join her and Jeff over Christmas, Jade had lied and said she was throwing a big Christmas yacht party for her friends.

Truth was she'd wanted to hunker down here and sob into her tequila over her crushed dreams with Beau. Not that the creep deserved one shed of her tears but still it hurt to think he could drop her so easily and move onto another woman. She thought she'd been in love with him. Now she knew better.

Besides, she hadn't wanted to intrude on Johnna and Jeff. After all, it was their first Christmas together after being married and next year they'd have a gorgeous baby.

The marina music drifted off to a Frosty the Snowman tune when Jade got the strangest fluttery feeling deep in the pit of her belly and the wildest feeling she was being watched.

Even before she could raise her head to look around and investigate, the sound of his deep voice sent shimmers of pleasure sliding over her flesh.

"Miss Jade Hart?"

She swallowed at the sound of his husky voice and looked up.

He stood on her gangplank.

All six feet plus of gorgeous, testosterone male.

Tight blue jeans were wrapped snugly around a nice torso and swaddled quite an impressive bulge between a set of powerful-looking legs.

His arms bulged with sleek muscles as he held onto a battered-looking tool case. He wore a simple white short-sleeved cotton shirt with the first few buttons undone to reveal a light dusting of curly dark chest hair. Black hair fluttered over a nice forehead and feathered loosely against his sides of his head. A gorgeous five o'clock stubble shadowed his face. Full kissable lips were upturned into a heart-clenching smile complete with bursting dimples in his cheeks and a deep cleft in his square chin.

At the delicious sight, a carnal tremor shimmered through her making her blood heat and her pussy scream in sexual awareness.

Wow! Hello handsome! Please fuck me now!

The hottest-looking pair of denim blue eyes squinted against the late afternoon sunshine, as he stared straight at her, well no, not at her exactly.

At her bare breasts!

Oh, shit!

She resisted the urge to cover herself and watched the pink tip of his tongue peek out from between his sensually shaped lips as he continued to watch her.

Gosh what she would do to feel this guy's hot mouth and wet tongue roaming over her breasts, lapping her nipples and licking the rest of her sex-deprived body.

At those delicious thoughts, her pussy moistened and Jade realized that in the way she was lying on the chaise, with both her legs pulled up and slightly parted he was probably getting a great view of her skimpy cloth-covered pussy.

Okay, just act natural. Act as if it was an everyday occurrence that she allowed a strange man to see her practically naked.

By golly, why wasn't she the least embarrassed by his appreciative gaze?

"Hi! I'm Jade Hart. May I help you?" she managed to squeak and quickly cleared her throat.

He blinked at the sound of her voice and she didn't miss the sweet pink flush that rushed over his cheekbones.

How cute! The man was embarrassed!

And she wasn't!

Wasn't this a lovely turn of events?

"Um... I um..." he stammered.

Jade's gaze zeroed in on the toolbox.

"You're the mechanic? To fix my engines?"

She'd called the marina asking them if they would send someone reliable over to fix the intermittent stalling problems the yacht had encountered when she'd taken her sisters out for a spin the other day.

The handyman cleared his throat.

"Yes ma'am. My name is Caydon. Caydon Minnelli. I brought my work references since I have never been here before." He placed some sheets of paper onto a nearby bench and set a life preserver on top.

"When you get a chance you can check and um... If you'll just tell me where your engine room is..."

She really should send him away until she could verify his references. Or at the very least, she should cover her breasts.

It was too dangerous to be alone with a strange man and her lying around half-naked. He might get the wrong idea.

But the cute way he kept glancing at her breasts was really turning her on.

Her stomach fell as his gaze dropped to where she'd hung her cane off a nearby deck table.

Who was she kidding? The man wouldn't even bother with her! She was practically handicapped. Her hip and leg were full of hideous scars from the surgeries. No man in his right mind would find her sexy.

Besides, since the accident, she'd packed on a good twenty pounds and here she was showing off her body. The only thing she'd get from this guy was him feeling sorry for her.

That's probably why she wasn't embarrassed at having him seeing her...because she was too busy feeling sorry for herself.

Loser girl!

Get a grip. The guy is here to fix the engines and nothing more.

Jade pointed to the cabin behind her and immediately noticed how her breasts jiggled at her movement.

Hmm. Maybe there was something good about her packing on those extra pounds after her accident. Her boobs weren't so small anymore. She hadn't realized it until just now.

Smiling inwardly at the way his Adam's apple bobbed when he swallowed, she kept her voice cool and professional as she spoke, "The stairs to the engine room are through those doors, through the kitchen, through the bedroom. You'll find the door to your right at the end of the hall."

He stood there for a moment, his gaze transfixed to her cane, an odd little frown on his cute face.

Her stomach plummeted.

See? He was already feeling sorry for her.

"When you're finished you can just send the bill to the marina...they'll forward it to me, if that's okay?"

He nodded, stepped onto her deck and quickly slipped past her without looking her way.

It gave her the encouragement to watch his long strides as he strolled across her cherry wood-paneled deck.

Despite her best efforts to still the sexual hunger flowing through her heated veins, her pulse went haywire at the sensual outline of his plump ass cheeks cupped by his jeans.

Wowsie! Nice ass.

When he disappeared through the door, Jade let out a long slow whistle.

She wouldn't mind running an exploring tongue along that butt or get a taste of his cock.

She let out a quick breath and wiped away the perspiration sprinkling across her forehead.

The man was one juicy-looking fellow!

Jade rolled her eyes in disappointment. A man built like him wouldn't be interested in her. It was best she just resign herself to the fact that the only reason he'd pay attention to her was because he thought she was loaded and she was paying his handyman bill.

Jade shook her head.

Sometimes having lots of money sucked.

As a child, she'd craved it. As a teenager, she'd trained for it. Now as an adult, she had it.

Unfortunately, having money produced lots of admirers. Admirers for her money, that is. That's the harsh lesson she'd learned from Beau.

Settling herself more comfortably in her white vinyl lounge chair, Jade resisted the urge to cover her breasts with her beach towel. She'd allow the sun to bathe her just like she'd been planning to do and when she heard him coming back she'd cover herself then.

She smiled to herself.

It sure had felt fantastic to have him looking at her the way he had. The hungry look in his eyes, the cute way his tongue had licked his lips as if he'd wanted to feast on her nipples, maybe even taste her down there?

She blushed at that thought.

Her sisters were right. It was time she got herself laid.

Maybe she should phone Jillian and ask her to express-courier another questionnaire?

Wouldn't that shock her sisters silly if shy Jade actually did mail a questionnaire to Kidnap Fantasies., and had herself a lovely fuck-fest with a stranger?

A burst of hammering from below deck shattered her thoughts.

It was quickly followed by silence.

The handyman was busy with his job and thankfully someone had finally shut off that blasted Christmas music.

Halleluiah!

Peace and quiet.

Jade closed her eyes and relaxed.

She let go of the Kidnap Fantasies brochure and it dropped with a plop to the deck.

A moment later, an easygoing whistling tune from the handyman drifted through the air.

Gosh, she hadn't heard a man whistle so softly before in her life.

Thankfully, it wasn't a Christmas song but an old Frank Sinatra song she hadn't heard in ages.

Her grandmother loved listening to Frank Sinatra.

Warm memories of Gram bustling in her kitchen filtered into her mind. She could still remember the cinnamon and allspice scents of her hot apple pies baking in the oven. The peppery sound of ice crystals and snow snapping against the windows of their home during the snowstorms they'd experience in upper New York state. Most of all she remembered how every Sunday afternoon Gram would put on the record player and play her favorite records.

Jade smiled into the memories. Gram was the sweetest woman in the world who'd always made her and her sisters feel so loved. So safe and secure.

The handyman's calm whistling slowly intermingled into her thoughts of Gram. She could practically hear dear Gram's soft voice, "It doesn't matter how rich or how poor the man is, base your decision on what your heart tells you. Nothing else matters..."

The gentle breeze tinged with the salty aroma of the ocean and the warm sunshine splashing over her practically nude body made her mind drift into a peaceful place she hadn't experienced in a very long time.

Before she knew it, she'd been lulled to sleep.

* * * * *

Caydon Minnelli smacked the hammer against the engine room's wooden floor one more time just for good measure. He had to make it sound like he was fixing her engines, didn't he?

Even if he was here for a totally different reason.

From what the team at Kidnap Fantasies had found out, Jade Hart was rich and a celebrity of sorts.

She'd won several gold medals at the Olympics and won a few Downhill Skiing World Cup Championships. Up until last year's tragic skiing mishap in Cortina d'Ampezzo, Italy, an accident many blamed on her coach, she'd been roaring toward the world's best professional skier position.

Gaining an impressive financial situation due to appearances in various commercials, she also had a signature jewelry line that a conglomerate ran for her and with some good sound investments; she was now a wealthy woman who didn't want for money.

Over the past year while she'd recuperated from her wipeout on a mountain slope, she'd written a tell-all tale about her childhood including the death of her parents at an early age and the tumultuous relationship with her ski coach of ten years.

A coach who'd pushed her mercilessly, conditioning her for the number one position in the skiing world. A coach who'd let her go out onto an icy slope for a trial run even when the authorities had warned everyone to stay off the slopes.

A disgusting coach who'd finagled his way into becoming her fiancé and who'd left her shortly after the tragic accident last year and moved on to coach and marry another famous millionaire skier.

Jade's autobiography titled Skiing in the Rain, released not too long ago, had once again put her in the spotlight.

Caydon's grip tightened on the hammer as remembered seeing her cane. Conflicting emotions had bombarded him. Anger, at wanting her ex-fiancé dead. Inkles of fear that she'd reject him at what he was planning to do with her. Most of all though he experienced a nice warm fuzzy feeling whenever he thought about her.

She'd looked so vulnerable lying there in the bright sunshine reading the Kidnap Fantasies brochure he'd given her sister to give to Jade.

His hungry gaze had roved over every inch of her body in mere seconds.

The instant he'd seen her tanned globes with the large suckable pink nipples nestled in large areolas, his mouth had watered at the thought of taking her flesh into his mouth and making her moan with erotic pleasure.

To his horror, his face had flushed with embarrassment when her gorgeous eyes had latched onto him and seen him ogling her. By golly, he hadn't been this shy near a woman since high school. Not to mention his cock hadn't reacted so powerfully since he was a teenager.

His equipment hardened, swelled and pulsed painfully against the tight restraints of his jeans, aching to burst through the zipper and slide into her pussy.

He hadn't missed her reaction either as he'd spied the wet spot of her arousal dotting her thong swim bottoms.

By god! The woman was even prettier than the pictures he'd seen of her.

He could tell she was tall by those long powerful-looking legs. And her hips were wide enough so he could grab onto her while he fucked her good and hard.

Her hair was a shoulder-length sandy gold, her lips a ripe red like freshly picked strawberries. She had a perfect nose, cheeks with a pretty dusting of freckles and delicious-looking naked earlobes he could nibble on all night.

Not to mention those gorgeous jade-colored eyes that had looked at him from behind a pair of sexy gold-rimmed glasses. It made his breath slam up in his lungs making it hard for him to breathe.

Jade Hart was an elegant piece of work. Nice and curvy in all the right places just like her boat, Jewel of the Sea.

When he'd walked along the docks with the smell of fish drifting through the air he'd been impressed by the gleaming black and white fiberglass hull and the shiny silver-colored railings of her yacht. He couldn't help but admire the elegant mix of wood decorating the interior as he'd walked through the kitchen. Teak walls with mahogany trim and red cherry-planked floors gave it a nautical air but the cotton canvas blinds that dressed the windows, the cherry curved countertops, the stainless steel pots hanging from the low ceiling and the denim blue slipcovers on the benches gave the boat a homey lived-in feel.

Then he'd seen her snug bedroom. Well maybe bedroom wasn't quite the word for it.

A seductress' haven sounded more appropriate. The walls were golden pine wood planks with tongue-and-groove white-planked ceilings. Lots of windows framed by delicate white lace gave for a great view of the marina loaded with stylish yachts, the turquoise-colored ocean and the handful of boats with billowing sails dotting the horizon.

Best of all, her bed was big enough for the two of them to tumble around freely while he made mad passionate love to her.

Caydon's lips tilted in a smile.

He sure was going to enjoy living in such close quarters with the pretty Jade Hart.

His smile quickly faded.

Now, if only he could get up enough nerve to carry out the rest of his plan.

Doubts crept into his thoughts and he gave a nearby pipe a frustrated whack.

Dammit! He'd never done something like this before.

Was he nuts coming here to seduce a virtual stranger?

Shit!

The answer was simple.

Yes. He was nuts.

Throwing the hammer down into the toolbox, he withdrew Jade Hart's Kidnap Fantasies questionnaire and began to read it for the umpteenth time.

The written words made his cock thicken and elongate. Within seconds his flesh pressed agonizingly against his pants, throbbing wildly, anticipating what was to come.

He inhaled a deep steadying breath and nodded to himself.

It was high time to gather his nerves, put his ass into gear and kidnap himself a woman.

Chapter Three

It wasn't the sound of the waves smacking against the hull of her yacht that drifted through Jade's many layers of sleep and alerted her to the fact something wasn't quite right. Nor was it the salty smell of cool ocean air that sent a shiver of alarm racing up her spine.

It was the lack of bell buoys clanging, the gentle rocking of her craft in obvious movement and the unmistakable zesty scent of tomato sauce drifting into her lungs that warned her something wasn't as it should be.

But how could that be? She was alone on her boat.

Alone...except for that handyman she'd let on board.

She forced her eyes open and blinked at the rosy-colored clouds sailing through the late afternoon blue sky unable to figure out where she was.

And then it hit her.

Sweet mercy! She'd fallen asleep. Drifted off while listening to that handyman whistling those Frank Sinatra melodies.

She noticed a beach towel had been draped over her naked breasts and a shiver of unease zipped through her.

Oh dear. She didn't remember doing that.

Shooting a glance at the railing and beyond she saw nothing but miles and miles of endless green ocean waves.

Not good!

A shot of adrenalin made her bolt upright into a seated position and she looked around.

There was no sign of him.

Heart hammering against her naked chest, she grabbed her nearby white silky swim cover-up and quickly shrugged into its softness. Tying the sash, she grabbed her cane and ignored the stiffness in her hip as she wrestled out of her chaise.

Where was that handyman? Had he left? Had the yacht somehow become disentangled from the security lines and drifted out of the marina? That would explain why she didn't hear the sound of engines.

How in the world did the boat get free? She always made sure the lines were secure. She'd need to get up to the pilothouse and swing the yacht around and head back to shore.

"Good evening!"

Shit!

The sound of the handyman's deep, masculine voice sent a shiver of nervousness racing up her back. Shielding her eyes against the late afternoon sunshine, she caught sight of his head poking out one of the kitchen windows. He leaned further out the window and waved at her.

Her pulse picked up speed as she noted his shirtless, tanned chest dotted with dark chest hair.

"What happened? Why are we out here?" she called to him, praying he'd give her a perfectly reasonable explanation.

"I didn't want to wake you so I took her out to see if I fixed the problem and...it died."

"It died?"

Her grip tightened on her cane. Oh! Please don't tell me this.

He elaborated by slicing a finger across his neck in a cutting his throat motion.

"Like in dead," he called out. "Looks like we're stranded out here for a little while. At least until after dinner."

Dinner? Was he nuts? She couldn't be stranded out here in the middle of the ocean with a stranger.

"I can radio for help!" Yes, that's what she'd do.

"I already did. The Coast Guard is tied up with a missing boat. I told them not to worry about us. It isn't an emergency. I can fix the problem...I think."

He thinks?

He smiled sheepishly. Those cute dimples burst into his cheeks making her pulse quicken despite her fear.

"They know where we are. In the meantime, come on over to the other deck. Dinner is just about ready. You are hungry, aren't you? I hate eating alone."

Dinner was almost ready? He hated eating alone? Bold fellow, wasn't he? A complete turnaround from the shy guy with the pink-tinged cheeks as he'd avoided looking at her breasts earlier.

"While you slept I took the liberty of whipping up some dinner for us. I hope you don't mind?"

God, yes she did mind. The man had her scared witless for heaven's sake.

"Um, that's fine," she said meekly.

"Come on!" He waved his arm again and Jade's mouth went dry at the sight of muscles rippling across his bare chest.

Is this guy for real?

Before she could protest, he poked his head back inside the cabin and was gone.

Now what should she do? It certainly would be highly embarrassing if she called for help and this guy was legit. Besides, if he were a killer or a rapist he sure wouldn't be cooking dinner for her. Would he?

The soft sound of his whistling "Rudolph the Red-Nosed Reindeer" reached her ears.

She nodded and squared her shoulders. Okay! She could handle this. Truly, she could.

Tightening her hold on her cane, Jade hobbled precariously until her stiff hip loosened and then she picked up her pace.

She'd march right into the galley and make him take her back to shore.

Well, that wouldn't work, would it? He'd just said the engines had died. Or had they? Could she trust him? Maybe he'd only told her that so he could...what?

Jump her bones?

As if he would want to screw a cripple, Jade thought wryly.

Don't be melodramatic, woman! He isn't the least bit interested in you.

Cautiously she headed toward the kitchen. The mouth-watering smell grew more pronounced as she drew closer.

Yes, she could definitely handle this guy. He was just a handyman. He had no ulterior motives. She was the one who kept thinking about him wanting to have sex with her. Not that she wouldn't mind jumping his bones and pulling down those tight jeans to get a good look at that lovely sized bulge he had hidden in there.

Jade shook her head.

This is what happens when you go too long without a man, she chided herself.

Gathering a breath, she pushed open the door and to her surprise found the small kitchen empty.

Where the heck did he go?

The mouth-watering smell of the tomato sauce teased her into the room. Passing the scaled-down marine fridge, she found a pot of boiling water and in another pot, sauce splashing all around the stainless steel stovetop.

She groaned inwardly. Not at the mess but at the yummy mouth-watering aroma.

She hadn't smelled something this delicious since before Gram had died.

Jade couldn't stop the smile from lifting her lips at the memory of her grandmother and at the way she'd enjoyed slaving over a hot stove on a cold winter day getting supper ready for her two sisters and herself after they'd spent a day of skiing.

"You like?"

She jumped in surprise at his voice and froze at the unmistakable bulge pressing ever so slightly against her ass.

Have mercy! The bulge felt exceptionally big and oh so hot and wonderfully hard. She felt a rush of moisture cream her pussy and her swimsuit bottom suddenly felt wet.

"Sorry, I didn't mean to scare you," he whispered and stepped around her.

Was he talking about the size of his cock frightening her?

No, he couldn't be. He was acting way too casual. As cool as a cucumber. Acting as if he hadn't just teased her with that hot swell. Or maybe that bulge had been her imagination?

As he stirred the sauce, her eyes drifted to the front of his jeans.

Jade groaned inwardly.

Oh dear!

The front of his jeans had indeed swelled wonderfully and she fought the impulse to slip her fingers into his jeans and bring out what must be a magnificent-sized cock.

Anticipation weakened her legs. She lifted her gaze to his naked chest.

God! What she wouldn't do to smooth her hands over those lovely rippling muscles or take his plump nipples into her mouth and bite those bronze pebbles.

Oh yes, and she wouldn't mind having this man go down on her.

As he stirred the sauce, she watched those long masculine fingers curl around the wooden stir stick and her ass ached to have his large hands smacking her sensitive bottom until her flesh blazed. She wanted to have those long fingers spreading her cheeks apart and welcoming his thick long cock into her tiny back hole.

Heavens!

It suddenly seemed a wee bit too warm in here. She needed an excuse to pop outside and suck in some cool ocean air.

"Why don't you head out to the back deck? Everything's ready."

Gosh! Was he reading her mind or what?

"Why are you doing this?" The words were out of her mouth before she could stop them.

He cocked a puzzled eyebrow at her. "Doing what? Cooking?"

No, making my hormones go haywire. Making me want you. Making me yearn for your hard cock plunging deep inside of me until I scream from orgasm after orgasm.

Oh boy.

She nodded, wishing away the flush of heat flooding her cheeks and trying to still the fear of an answer she didn't want to hear. Like maybe, he was a serial killer. Like maybe, he wanted to fatten her up before he killed her.

"I like to cook."

Simple enough answer.

So why didn't she believe him?

"Why?" he asked softly. "Did you think I kidnapped you?"

His words hung heavy in the air as he awaited her answer. Obviously, he'd seen the Kidnap Fantasies brochure that she'd dropped onto the deck before nodding off.

Had he read it while she'd slept? Had that brochure given him some naughty ideas?

Oh, my gosh! Wouldn't that be something? Kidnapped by the handyman.

"No, of course not, don't be silly," she lied.

Have mercy but if she hadn't misplaced that questionnaire she would have asked for a guy just like this one.

He smiled, broke eye contact and returned his attention to his sauce.

"Grub's just about ready. Have yourself a seat on the back deck."

The guy was making himself quite at home, wasn't he? Cooking supper without a shirt. Wrecking her boat's engines. Stranding them out here in the middle of nowhere. Looking hot and sexy in a tight pair of jeans. Pressing his gorgeous cock against the crack of her ass. Making her crave him.

Jade did what he suggested. On shaky legs, she made her way out of the kitchen and past her bedroom with the ominous cane clicking loudly against the polished cherry-planked floor.

When she emerged outside, the warm salty ocean air kissed her face, but it did nothing to dampen the heat uncurling deep in her ass where he'd pressed ever so slightly against her, nor did it stop the fire that had unraveled deep inside her pussy.

She blinked in surprise at the sight in front of her.

He'd set the small deck table with her nicest tablecloth complete with the white linen napkins and the silver cutlery she'd inherited from Gram.

A lone candle perched inside a candleholder flickered in the middle of the table. Chilling inside the ice bucket sat a bottle of wine. And set on the far side of the table were his reference papers.

What in the world? If she didn't know any better she'd think he was trying to get her to trust him with his papers and prepared this romantic dinner to set a scene for a seduction.

Jade's pulse hammered at that thought.

Could this handyman actually want to have sex with her?

This time she smelled his clean male scent even before his masculine heat caressed her back as he came up behind her.

"You like?" His blue eyes seemed to shine with lust as he held a large dish full of tomato sauce-laden spaghetti.

Her pulse skittered.

"Yes, it's very pretty." No way was she going to say it was a romantic scene for a seduction. After all, she could be reading this all wrong.

He set the dish onto the table and to her surprise; he pulled out a deck chair for her. "Have a seat."

Quite aware that she was topless beneath her cover-up, she hesitated.

"Um, maybe I should go and get dressed for dinner."

He grinned and her belly did a wonderful somersault. His smile was so friendly and sexy.

"You're perfect the way you are. Please, sit. Enjoy the view while I get us the rest."

Oh, she was enjoying the view all right, she thought as she sat down. She watched his cute ass sway against his tight jeans as he went back inside.

When he disappeared, she shook her head.

What in the world was she going to do? What if he was setting a scene for a seduction? Could she go through with it?

But what if the way he'd pressed his cock against her backside had been a mistake? Maybe he'd accidentally brushed against her and he hadn't even noticed?

Jade swallowed her nervousness. She'd noticed and she wanted more.

Much more.

She reached out and removed a paperweight then grabbed his papers. A quick glance at the names revealed he'd done work for plenty of people she knew. Some of them were her good friends. Their personal cell numbers were accurate. Not just anyone would have access to those numbers because they were famous and didn't give out their personal numbers to just anyone. It appeared he truly could be trusted.

She breathed a heavy sigh of relief, closed her eyes and said a silent prayer of thanks.

A moment later, she opened her eyes just in time to watch him show up with a large dish of raw vegetables.

He'd raided her pantry!

As her gaze raked over the phallus-shaped raw eggplant, the thick short carrots, and the long slender cucumbers, she remembered writing down on that Kidnap Fantasies questionnaire about having a fantasy about doing it with vegetables but truly never had had the nerve.

Her momentary excitement plummeted when she spotted a peeler and the vegetable dip set in the middle of the dish.

"I know some women prefer their vegetables raw," he said as he set the dish on the table and looked down at her.

He nodded to the steaming bowl of spaghetti. "So? What do you think? Do you like my culinary expertise?"

She nodded and set his references back onto the table where she'd found them, then settled the weight on top, preventing them from flying away in the breeze.

"I must have been asleep for quite some time for you to whip all this up."

He winked at her and sat down beside her.

"In the way you were smiling in your sleep I didn't want to disturb you."

To her shock, her face heated at the thought of his hot gaze roving over her naked breasts while she'd slept.

In the breeze, his dark hair fluttered and his silky-looking chest muscles jerked wonderfully as he scooped a couple of healthy helpings of the delicious-looking spaghetti onto her plate.

"Dig in. Tell me what you think."

Gosh, she was sitting here beside a gorgeous hunk who was feeding her spaghetti and all she could do was blush?

Fuck me! Her mind shouted at him.

Her mouth didn't participate with her thoughts and she shoved a forkful of spaghetti past her lips. Scrumptious flavor burst against her taste buds. She closed her eyes and moaned her approval.

"Sounds good," his voice sounded husky.

Was he talking about the way she'd just moaned? Or the way she'd just...moaned...like in a sexual way?

She snapped her eyes open to catch him watching her in such a way that made her feel vulnerable and scared.

Vulnerable because she could easily fall for a guy who'd actually cook supper for her and scared that she was reading way too much into this.

He nodded at her bowl. "C'mon, eat it all up."

You can eat me anytime, Jade thought as she swallowed the food and tried to act natural.

"I haven't had spaghetti this good since before my grandmother died. You must give me your recipe." She would have her cook whip up a batch for her when she got back to Los Angeles.

"Actually it is a secret family recipe but I'll tell it to you. Wine. A healthy dose of wine to canned tomatoes and spices. Lots of basil, sage, thyme."

He shoved a healthy forkful into his mouth.

"Mmm, very good if I do say so myself." He wiggled his dark eyebrows at her in Groucho Marx style and she laughed and relaxed a little.

She had to be reading too much into this guy. He wasn't interested in her. He was probably feeling guilty for stranding them out here, had simply cooked up a meal because he was hungry and she'd been asleep.

Twirling her fork, she gathered up more of the delicious spaghetti and continued to eat. Each bite seemed more succulent than the previous one. Before she knew it, she'd totally relaxed and helped herself to seconds.

"Is there anyone you should contact? Anyone waiting for you at home? I mean it'll be Christmas Eve tomorrow..." she said trying hard to appear casual as she dabbed sauce from the corners of her lips with one of her grandmother's linen napkins.

"You're asking if I'm married or have a girlfriend. The answer is no. Not at the moment. And no one is expecting me this year for Christmas festivities. Unless you consider a fern that my mom gave me because she

thought I'd need some oxygen in the big stuffy house I live in. Wine?"
he asked as his big hand picked up the bottle.

She admired the length of his fingers as they curled around the
stem of a glass. Oh yes, nice long thick fingers. Perfect for fucking her
aching pussy.

"What about your family?"

"A toast," he cut her off, and handed her the glass and then held his
up. "To...a very Merry Christmas and a Happy New Year."

"A Merry Christmas," Jade whispered as his warm gaze held hers.
She wasn't sure about the upcoming New Year being happy, so she
remained silent.

Their glasses clinked together.

It was a cheerful sound. A sound she hadn't heard in quite some
time.

"My family can survive without me this year," he grinned.

She sipped her wine trying hard not to read too much into his
comment or that gorgeous smile that was making her toes curl as she
watched the sexual way his lips arched over his glass while he drank the
ruby liquid. She wouldn't mind tasting the sensual curves of his mouth.
Wouldn't mind having his hot lips sucking on her clit the way he was
doing that glass.

Oh dear, she needed to get her thoughts onto something else.

"You said your last name is Minnelli?"

He nodded.

"Italian?"

"My grandparents are from northern Italy."

Northern Italy.

A cold familiar tightness clamped over her chest. That's where she'd
taken the horrible fall on the icy slope during last year's training run.

"You're not smiling anymore. Something I said?"

Concern etched his features and he placed his wineglass upon the
table.

"No, it's nothing."

"Tell me," the softness in his voice soothed her. Made her want to share what she'd gone through over the past year.

"It was in Italy where I broke my hip and leg."

"Ah yes, your skiing accident."

Jade blinked in shock. "You know about that?"

"I've seen your pictures in the magazines. I recognized your name. I've been an admirer of yours since you started professionally skiing."

"Oh." So he knew she was rich, too. Was that why he was interested in her? Was he like Beau? Looking for an easy buck?

His toe nudged against her bare foot. "You're still frowning."

She looked down and realized he'd slipped his shoes off.

He had big feet.

Big feet. Big cock.

Oh boy! Her thoughts were turning to that again. Was it any wonder? With a gorgeous, bare-chested man sitting right beside her.

"So why were you out on the slope that day? I'd read everyone had been told to stay off of it."

"Apparently someone forgot to tell me."

"Meaning your coach...your fiancé."

"Ex-fiancé," she said coldly, the familiar anger churning up inside her. "It wasn't really his fault. He was too busy kissing up to a new blonde bombshell ski supplier that morning. When I asked him if it was okay to go out on the slopes he merely nodded. Thinking back on it I don't think he'd heard a word I'd said. I should have checked the conditions myself before going out."

"But your coach did that stuff for you. So you had no way of knowing about it."

Irritation snapped through her. Exactly how much did he know about her?

"Why are we talking about this? How do you know about what my coach's responsibilities are?"

"Like I said, I'm an admirer and I also read your book."

Shit!

"So you pretty much know everything about me then." She fingered the moisture droplets forming on her wineglass. Wondered if maybe he just might be one of those paparazzi who'd tracked her down.

"Not everything. But I'd like to find out."

Her head snapped up at the soft way he said it.

She caught that sexy smile that made her toes curl. His teeth gleamed white and she fought the impulse of wanting to smooth her tongue across them.

"For instance?" she asked.

He grabbed the biggest carrot from the vegetable tray and examined it carefully.

"I remember reading you eat vegetables from your own vegetable garden."

Her throat went dry at the way his finger tenderly stroked the long thick carrot. His eyes sparkled with amusement and lust.

"That's right."

"And you enjoy physical labor."

Her heart was beating so loud now that she was sure he could hear it too.

"Depends on what type," she whispered.

His smile widened and he nodded to the quickly darkening horizon. "Looks like a good night to spend out on the ocean."

Was that an invitation? Or merely an observation?

She followed his gaze and inhaled at the pale pink blooming clouds tinting the baby blue skyline.

"I haven't seen something this breathtaking in a very long time," she agreed.

"Neither have I." His voice sounded too husky for her not to catch his meaning.

She looked over at him.

Lust shone darker in his eyes as he looked at her.

"I've been wanting to taste you from the moment I saw you, Jade Hart. Taste all of you," he whispered.

All of her?

Her pulse skittered and her pussy quivered in anticipation.

His words stunned her. The intense way he looked at her shocked her.

He leaned closer. His rich masculine scent devoured her senses. A mental image popped into her head. An image of her handyman lowering himself between her legs, the heavy weight of her body pinned beneath him, his strong muscles flattening against her softness, his engorged cock plunging into her.

If that bulge she'd felt pressed against her backside was an indication she was in for quite a ride. Her vaginal muscles spasmed and she swallowed at a tinge of nervousness of maybe not being able to accommodate his size.

Her gaze drew to his face, to his succulent-looking mouth that was now opening.

Her lips tingled in anticipation.

Oh, my gosh! She'd been right.

He had pushed his cock up against her backside on purpose. He'd been checking for her reaction. Checking to see if his size would frighten her.

Her eyes closed the instant his mouth touched hers. All thoughts flew into the ocean breeze.

Fire puffed through her mouth as hot lips brushed against hers. He tasted of ice-wine, tomato sauce and raw man.

What a magnificent combination!

His breathing was harsh and his lips tightened over hers, holding her captive.

A little growl of pleasure escaped his throat. It was a sound she'd never heard before from a man. A sexy sound that made her vaginal muscles tremble wonderfully.

Suddenly she couldn't get close enough to him. Her hands slipped around his neck pulling him deeper into the kiss.

Eager masculine fingers fought with the sash on her cover-up. Mild ocean air brushed against her bare shoulders as the robe slipped away.

Warm calloused hands palmed her breasts.

Oh gosh, that feels so good.

She pressed herself into his hands. Her breasts swelled beneath his fingers as he began a slow erotic massage. She hadn't had a man touch her like this in so long. Hadn't ever had a man kiss her so hard and with such confidence.

His moist mouth slid against hers, licking at her bottom lip, biting sweetly until she couldn't resist but to open to him.

He came in hard and he came in fast.

Teeth scraped against teeth. His scorching tongue slid quickly over the upper row of her teeth and gums, exploring every detail before pushing into her to tangle mercilessly with her tongue.

He kissed her like a man possessed. His quick tongue shot deep thrusts into her mouth, keeping her mind off balance.

His fingers squeezed at her nipples. Sweet pain seared her breasts and he caught her cry in his mouth. Fevered heat spread outward from her lower abdomen.

It felt incredible.

Suddenly he pulled away.

In the sunset, his eyes were dark, his mouth shone red and gleamed wet from their kiss.

Heat brewed in his eyes and she liked the sweetly dangerous expression on his face as he stared at her bared breasts.

"Your breasts are breathtaking. Nipples so large that a man's mouth would have a feast making love to them."

Oh my gosh! No guy had ever said that to her before.

His large hands tightened around her breasts, making them appear bigger and more swollen.

"Absolutely beautiful," he whispered.

Her eyes widened with surprise as he lowered his head. He opened his mouth and his moist lips greedily latched onto her plump nipple.

A soft moan escaped her throat as spirals of pleasure zipped along her flesh. He sucked her bud into the hot interior of his mouth as if it were a delicious red cherry.

Beneath his ministrations, she trembled. His teeth nibbled on her quivering bud. She lifted her hands from his neck and placed them on both sides of his head, sifting her fingers through his feathery hair and inhaling the sexy scent of man.

Arching her back, she pressed her swollen breast into his face. The five o'clock stubble surrounding his lips scratched her flesh. Erotic fervor shifted wonderful warmth through her lower belly. Her pussy tightened into a wild burn.

He drank at her nipple. His tongue swirled around her areole, lighting her flesh on fire. Firm masculine hands trailed along her sides to caress the curves of her hips. Sweet sucking sounds drifted through the air. The sensual movements of his tongue laved her nipple igniting quivers deep inside her pussy.

Heated moisture pooled into her swimsuit panties.

Drawing away from her swollen nipple, he attached his moist eager mouth to the other quivering bud. He sucked with so much enthusiasm Jade couldn't stop herself from throwing her head back and moaning her pleasure.

The man was good. Very good.

The scent of her arousal drifted up from between her legs and mingled with the salty scent of sea air. It was an aroma that blended deliciously together.

She wondered what he was thinking, as he smelled her arousal. Wondered how far he wanted to go. Wondered how far she would allow him to go.

Desire raged at the idea that she wanted him to go all the way.

A one-night stand. No strings sex.

She could free herself in his arms tonight. She could get him to do things to her that she'd always wanted done. She'd never have to see him again. She'd never have to be embarrassed.

She eyed the bowl of vegetables with longing, her anticipation mounting.

With a pop, he let go of her nipple and buried his face in the valley between her breasts.

His breath came hard and fast. Aroused. Shaky.

Like hers.

"Don't stop," she whispered.

She wanted more from him. Wanted him to unleash her carnal side.

God! Her sisters had been right. She needed a good stiff fucking. And she needed it bad.

His hands slid away from her hips.

A moment later, burning fingers curled over her knees.

"Open." His word was muffled as he kissed the valley between her breasts.

She hesitated.

Fantasies were fantasies. This man was real. Could she open her legs to a complete stranger?

"Open wide, Jade," he prodded.

This time he spoke with a sweet firmness that sent a tingle of fear skittering up her spine. What would he do to her if she protested? Would he tie her down? Would he take her against her will?

Her pussy clenched at those thoughts.

She was so tempted to find out. So tempted to live dangerously.

But what if she denied him and he stopped doing what he was doing? She didn't want him to stop. She'd never had a man touch her with such heat in his hands.

He made her feel like a woman.

Heart beating rapidly against her chest, she opened her legs wide to him.

He pulled his head away from her breasts. Within a split second, he sank onto his knees in front of her.

His gaze scorched her pussy as he stared between her legs. His hot look made her pulse race.

Oh my gosh!

"You're soaked," he growled. His voice sounded strangled.

"It happens when a man kisses me," she replied unsure if she was saying the right thing.

His eyes narrowed at her words. A brief flash of anger zipped through his eyes. Did she detect jealousy? It made her tremble with excitement.

"I bet many men have kissed you but not where I'm going to."

His voice had lost the softness. His gaze had a determined hard edge to it. That tingle of fear slithered into her again. This time she got the feeling if she protested he wouldn't stop.

Her thoughts spun.

This was happening way too fast. But there was no denying the heat searing her pussy. No denying she wanted him between her legs.

Long masculine fingers slid along the curve of her generous hips, curling beneath her thong bottom. As he drew the thin material down over her hips, she eagerly lifted her ass allowing him to pull off the thong.

"Touch your breasts," he whispered.

His eyes were intent, his voice a strong command.

Feeling a bit clumsy and suddenly shy, she cupped her hands over her breasts and began to massage herself the way she did when she masturbated.

"Watch me while you do it, Jade."

A scorching quiver of excitement rocked her. She did what he asked and kept her eyes drawn to his face.

"Pinch your nipples. Like the way I did to you earlier. Nice and hard. I want to see the pain flash in your eyes."

She did as he asked loving the fierce way he watched her every move.

Plucking her hard buds until her nipples ached, she grimaced at the pleasure-pain.

His blue eyes sparkled with approval when she finally cried out.

"That's it, Jade. Keep doing it while I tend to other business."

Before she could comprehend his meaning, his head lowered to the area between her legs.

Oh God! She couldn't believe this was happening. A man was actually going down on her!

The heat of his hands seeped into her flesh as he clasped her hips tighter. His face burrowed between her legs and a hot whisper of his breath teased her clit. The sight of a man's head between her legs was enough to almost make her climax on the spot.

His mouth covered her entire clit making her jolt against him. She pinched her nipples harder.

His hot tongue split her plump lips apart and flitted around her engorged clit in tiny circles, building a hungry sexual tension that made her moan out loud.

Her body throbbed. Her pussy pulsed. Her nipples poked hard against her hands. A magnificent quivering blossomed and she forced herself to remain in control.

A hot tongue slid into her drenched channel, stretching her. The heated length of his tongue burrowed into her like a stick of molten steel.

Her legs trembled. Her bad hip ached but it was a good ache. Her thighs tightened around his head and she squeezed.

Hard.

His tongue found her G-spot. He massaged her firmly there, stroking the sensitive area repeatedly making her shudder.

An euphoric haze embraced her and Jade gasped.

Her swollen breasts jiggled beneath her warm hands. Her nipples ached and throbbed as she continued to pinch herself. The gratifying pain shot lightning arrows between her thighs adding pleasure there.

His tongue zipped out of her vagina and he vigorously lapped at her clit. Sucking sounds sang through the cool ocean air. Blood roared in her ears and she wiggled against his torturous movements.

God help her but having a man's head between her thighs, the tension of a tongue spearing her vagina, the frantic touch of a man's lips suckling her labia was better than any fantasy she could have dreamed.

He sucked at her clit harder.

Her breathing grew labored. She continued to plump her aching nipples.

His tongue impaled her.

Spasms wrapped around her.

She threw her head back and cried out at the onslaught. She clenched her teeth and let go of her breasts, blindly grabbing his shoulders and grinding her hips against him.

White-hot fragments of pleasure scorched her. Her pussy muscles clenched his tongue. She gasped for air, kept her hips slamming into his face.

The orgasm rocked her. Tortured her. Relieved her.

Yes!

When the spasms ebbed, she slumped against the chair, perspiration dotting her skin.

Her breasts felt swollen. Her pussy pulsed with aftereffect spasms. Her eyes stayed closed. Her breaths came harsh and shallow.

He picked her up in his strong arms.

She didn't care where he was taking her. All she wanted was to bask in her sexual exhaustion.

Cool vinyl pressed against her back. Soft material of a beach towel drifted over her warm body.

"That was just the appetizer. I'll be back soon," he promised.

Oh God!

She nodded. At least she thought she nodded. Then she drifted away into blissful nothingness.

Chapter Four

He'd seduced her!

It had been so easy. Of course, it helped to be sexually attracted to her.

As he stood at the railing of her yacht looking out at the pristine mirror-like ocean, his legs trembled and his body screamed with sexual tension.

Reaching down, he unzipped his jeans, slid open his briefs and allowed his sore cock to spring free. The entire length burst forward, angry and raw, long and thick, heavy and hurting.

Damn, his cock had never ached so badly. Had never throbbed so much. He swore his balls would burst.

Reaching down he tenderly stroked his erection until the veins throbbed beneath his fingertips.

Unfortunately, his gentle stroking didn't ease him at all. It just aroused him more.

Gritting his teeth in frustration, he let go of his hard shaft and curled his hands around the metal railing allowing the cool ocean air to wash against his flaming shaft.

He knew he could bring himself relief in a mere few seconds. That's how primed and ready he was. He'd done it numerous times in the recent past but now he had Jade.

Beautiful.

Soft.

Sexy Jade.

If he went to her now, with this fiery need to fuck her with uncontrollable thrusts, he would most likely hurt her with his size.

Her channel was tight. Maybe too tight.

That's why he'd tongue-fucked her first. So he could explore her silky wetness to see if he'd fit. He'd savored the way her vaginal muscles had frantically gripped him.

His mind had screamed for him to pull out his burning cock and ram into her slit. But the fear of hurting her had stopped him.

Besides, her sweet cream had been intoxicating as he sipped from her vagina. The velvety flesh of her inner thighs had pressed against his head keeping him a willing captive between her luscious legs.

He smiled as he remembered the events leading up to his tongue-fucking Jade.

When he'd finally gathered the nerve to come out of the hold, he'd found her fast asleep on the lounge chair, a very pretty smile curving her lips.

While he'd gazed at her fully exposed breasts, his mouth had watered at the cherry sized nipples. Heated blood had rushed straight into his shaft, hardening his flesh until it seared like a long tight piece of molten steel making him cry out from the pleasurable sensations.

At the sound of his voice, she'd moved in her sleep, her legs widening as if she knew he was there standing over her. As if she'd wanted him to do her while she slept.

His blood had pumped feverishly through his entire body as he'd once again spotted the wetness dotting the thong.

He'd wanted to rip the tiny garment off her right then and there while she'd slept. Had wanted to push his heavy cock into her soaked pussy and then wake her so she'd find out she'd just been impaled.

He wanted to fuck her brains out.

But first, he wanted to romance her. Wine and dine her and not just have the wild sex she'd so liberally filled out in the Kidnap Fantasies questionnaire.

Instead of following his cravings, he'd draped the protection of the beach towel over her body and headed into the yacht's pilothouse.

He'd found the key on a hook beneath the console exactly where he'd been told it would be. He'd jammed the key into the ignition and looked out the crystal-clear windows down onto the gleaming cherry wood main deck where she lay stretched out on the chaise.

He'd twisted the key and the engines had roared to life. She hadn't moved.

Pushing the throttle forward, he'd slowly eased the yacht out of the marina and headed for open water.

She still hadn't budged. She was sleeping through her own kidnapping!

He'd almost laughed out loud at that thought.

Now he had himself a sexual captive and free rein of a delicious-looking sex-starved woman with the ocean as their playground.

He should be enjoying himself.

Yet, instead of telling her he'd just kidnapped her and was going to make all her fantasies come true, he'd chickened out.

Instead, he'd cooked her dinner and tongue-fucked her.

Shit!

He should tell her the real reason he was here. Tell her about Kidnap Fantasies. Tell her he'd come here because of the questionnaire he'd been given.

Peering over his shoulder, Caydon gazed at Jade who lay where he'd left her on the lounge, her luscious body hidden beneath a beach towel.

She'd awakened from her sexual stupor.

Her eyes were open as she stared into the now dark sky. Beneath the beach towel, he could tell her knees were lifted and he wondered if she was touching herself, toying with that plump clit, squeezing her puffy labia, sliding her fingers into her tight channel.

A blade of lust clenched his rock-hard balls and cock as he watched her. The blade twisted beautifully, making him want to show her exactly what she did to him.

From the moment he'd been given her picture by Kidnap Fantasies, it had been a dream come true. He hadn't lied when he'd told her he'd followed her career. He enjoyed watching professional downhill skiing. He'd read her autobiography and he knew Jade was special.

She was a giving, trusting person.

Innocent in sex.

According to quick research through Kidnap Fantasies, she'd been intimate with one man. Her ski coach who'd managed to become her fiancé.

Caydon intended to amend that situation. He planned to show her just how special she was but he hadn't missed the fear burst in her eyes a split second before he'd kissed her. The fear of getting hurt—fear of trusting him.

It would be natural for her to be afraid of him. He was a stranger, a man who'd made her dinner and taken her delicious nipples and her hot quivering pussy into his mouth for desert.

And he'd barely gotten started.

His heart crashed in his ears as he quietly approached her.

Her lush naked body looked relaxed in the moon glow. Her plump breasts moved up and down beneath the towel in a steady rhythm as she breathed. He could tell she was fingering herself, toying with her plump little clit. Maybe wanting another mouth-induced orgasm.

He should tell her right now about Kidnap Fantasies. That he had her questionnaire.

And when he did tell her?

Would she still enjoy the pleasures he'd bring to her? Or would she insist she wasn't interested in any more sex with him?

Without warning, her hand flew out from beneath the beach towel giving him a cock-clenching view of her generous breast and hardened nipple as she pointed to the sky.

"Falling star!" she cried out. "Make a wish!"

It only took him a split second to see the silver streak flash in the darkness and he quickly made his wish. The star disintegrated and Jade grew quiet again.

He noted the wistful smile playing on her sensually shaped lips. Lips meant for kissing. Lips meant for sucking cock.

His shaft tightened making him groan.

His breathing sounded harsh and fast in the semi-darkness.

He saw her body tense ever so slightly as he drew closer. She'd heard him, but she didn't look his way. Didn't see his angry cock sticking out of his pants wanting her so bad it trembled in anticipation of sinking into her.

"Let me look at your body, Jade," he whispered.

Her throat moved as she swallowed. She hesitated momentarily and then she pulled the beach towel off her body and let it drop to the floor.

Her nipples were still peaked, aroused. Her breasts swollen and full.

"Touch yourself, Jade. I want to watch." He enjoyed watching her touch herself. It turned him on.

A hand slid up her slightly rounded belly to her right breast. Her fingers tweaked at her nipple. Her other hand slid between her legs moving slowly as she stroked her clit.

"What did you wish for?" he asked.

She smiled coyly and shook her head.

"I can't tell you."

"Don't tell me you believe in that silly old wives' tale where if you tell someone your wish it won't come true, do you?"

She nodded. "You can tell me your wish if you want but I still won't tell you mine...unless it comes true."

"You sound doubtful it will."

She frowned and his heart tightened with sadness.

"My grandmother always said wishing upon a star would bring magic into my life. I always believed what she said was true. When I first bought this boat a couple of years back I used to sit out here in the dark and make lots of wishes but now I don't make them anymore."

"You just did. What's changed?"

She shrugged her bare shoulders and he noticed the wetness on her fingers as she slid her hand away from between her legs.

"Don't stop touching yourself."

Her eyes widened with shyness at his remark yet her hand slid between her legs again and he could see her fingering her clit.

"The scars don't bother you?" she whispered.

He hadn't really noticed them but now that she mentioned it he noticed several long lines along her thigh and hip areas. Obviously, she was self-conscious about them.

"Why? Should they bother me?"

"They're ugly. I thought about plastic surgery but I really don't want any more surgeries for awhile."

"Your scars are a part of you, Jade. At least they are for now. And I like everything I see about you."

"And so far I like everything about you, too," she said timidly.

"Look at me, Jade," he instructed. It was time to introduce her to another one of her fantasies.

Her head swung around to look at him and she blinked in surprise. The surprise quickly turned to shock, which was quickly followed by fear when she discovered the mushroom-shaped head of his long, thick ten-inch cock a foot away from her mouth.

"You don't have to if you don't want to." His voice sounded strangled and hopeful.

"I...do want to. Very much."

He noticed the tremble in her voice. Saw pink blush breeze across her cheeks. The fear in her eyes was gone, replaced by interest.

And desire.

Suddenly he felt nervous. Nervous at the things he'd planned for her, things that when she'd written them on paper might sound better to her than when she actually experienced it.

His anxiety quickly disappeared when she parted her sensually shaped lips. Lips still red and swollen from their earlier kiss.

With both hands, he held onto the base of his cock and could barely push the tip of his bulging flesh into her eager mouth before her lips clamped around his flesh.

Heated moisture sizzled around his cock and shot down his shaft straight into his tight balls.

His knees weakened at the impact and he almost exploded right then and there.

Gritting his teeth, he stifled a groan and held his ground.

Damn! Her mouth felt so good.

So tight. So velvety hot.

His entire body stiffened as the hot tip of her tongue poked tenderly at the slit in his cock-head.

Her hands began to move away from their respective places on her body but he didn't want that.

"No, Jade. I want you to keep touching yourself."

He wanted her to stay aroused while she tended to him. Wanted her wet and ready for him.

She did as he instructed, her fingers toying with her plump nipples, her other hand remaining between her velvety legs, moving slowly back and forth as she massaged her clit. Her breasts looked big and hard beneath the moonlight, her chest heaving with her heavy excited breaths.

With not even a quarter of his engorged cock disappearing between her luscious lips, her hair all tangled and messed up, eyes bright with lust, she looked like a sweet sexy angel.

His erection throbbed madly at the sight.

"Suck me, Jade. Suck me hard."

Her heated lips squeezed his cock as if it were in a vise and she began a slow caress around his engorged flesh, her hot little tongue laving his aching head making his balls constrict painfully.

A razor blade of pleasure zipped up his shaft making his breath catch.

He thrust his hips forward, pushing himself deeper into her mouth, wanting more of this agonizing joy.

She whimpered as his cock hit the back of her throat.

He withdrew slightly and curled his hand around his cock making sure not to go beyond that point.

The last thing he wanted to do was hurt her when he lost control.

Velvety cheeks slid against his hard rod. Sucking sounds split the air.

The pressure of her moist mouth sucking on his rigid flesh overwhelmed him, made him desperate for release. When her tongue began a mad circling around the head of his cock, he couldn't stop the groan of pleasure.

She whimpered in answer.

It was a beautiful sound that made his heart leap with warmth.

Pleasure rushed along his shaft. His hand clenched tighter around the base of his cock as he watched her continue to toy with her breast, rolling her nipple between her fingers until he saw the beautiful flash of pain in her eyes.

Her other hand moved quicker between her legs as she rubbed her clit. He could hear the slurping sounds of her fingers sliding in and out of her vagina.

Heat consumed his flesh as his orgasm built.

Closing his eyes, he remembered how she tasted when he'd taken her orally. Her hot, pulsing pleasure button had been stiff in his mouth. Her cum tasting sweet and innocent. Her throaty cries had sifted through the air warming his heart.

Now it was his turn to cry out as her mouth worked its wondrous magic.

Her lips gave his cock a hard squeeze, and Caydon's shaft rippled in ecstasy making him inhale sharply.

His heart thundered in his ears. His body screamed for relief. His self-control washed away in the lusty sensations.

The orgasm took over.

He groaned at the onslaught of pleasure.

"I'm coming!" he cried out as lusty lightning blades shimmered along his shaft and slammed into his heavy scrotum.

His balls burst.

Spurt after spurt he shot his sperm down her throat. Her lips tightened around his swollen cock sealing him as if she wanted to make sure he wouldn't withdraw or that she didn't miss a drop.

She sucked harder. The vibrations racing through his cock were unbelievable.

He cried out as she continued to milk him with her mouth.

Finally, when his cock went somewhat limp he withdrew and stared down at her.

She was a beautiful creature.

Eyes sparkled with passion. Her heart-shaped face was flushed, her parted lips swollen.

His body shuddered at the erotic sight.

Without a doubt, he knew what he wanted to do next.

* * * * *

"You give head beautifully."

"Thank you," Jade whispered.

Her face flamed in the darkness as he nestled onto the chaise beside her.

What had just happened between them was making her thoughts wobble all over the place and her body yearn for more sex. Taking a strange man's powerful cock into her mouth had always been one of her fantasies. She'd even wanted to take Beau orally but he'd pushed her away from him as if her wanting to suckle his cock was a disgusting act. She'd never tried again.

But the instant she'd spotted Caydon's large cock hovering like a stiff pole in front of her face, the intricate weave of angry veins pulsing along a thick shaft begging for relief she'd wanted to take him into her mouth.

She'd been surprised that she hadn't noticed him standing so close with his erection sticking out of his pants pleading for her attention. Fear had quickly followed at the sight of his shaft. Fear that maybe he wouldn't enjoy what she wanted to do to his cock. But that had quickly vanished, followed by an intense need to have him in her mouth.

He'd felt awesome. His blistering heated length had sunk deep into her, banging against her tonsils making her gag and she'd panicked.

When he'd retreated and allowed her full rein, she'd relaxed.

Allowing her lips to wrap around his hard velvety cock, she tightened her hold on him. Her tongue had laved and explored the mushroom-shaped head.

She'd tasted the salty pre-cum from his slit.

Had enjoyed it. Had wanted more.

Now her lips felt bruised, and swollen and oh so ready to suck him off again.

But what she craved even more at the moment was him driving his succulent cock deep into her wet pussy.

"You are beautiful woman, Jade. I can't get enough of looking at you." He nuzzled her earlobe with his firm lips sending sweet shivers racing down her spine.

"Despite my cane, you mean?" She couldn't keep the self-pity out of her voice. Couldn't stop herself from wanting him to reassure her that he truly did find her desirable as a woman.

"It gives you a damsel in distress quality. A quality I find enticing. It makes me want to protect you. Like I'm your knight in shining armor. Like you're vulnerable, totally at my mercy writhing beneath me as I fuck you long and hard."

Her breath caught at his seductive voice.

As he brushed his lips along her neck, she felt the hard outline of his fierce cock push against her naked hip.

Sweet heavens! The man was as hard as a rock already.

"You're such a sexy woman. I want you again."

She gasped in disappointment as he moved off the lounge. The disappointment didn't last long as his warm hands slipped underneath her, one beneath her knees, the other under her waist.

Scooping her into his arms, he stood. His body felt solid and deliciously feverish against her flesh as he began to walk.

"Where...where are we going?"

He flicked his lusty gaze down at her. "To your bedroom."

Heated blood coursed through her veins as he held her tightly in his arms. His hard chest scraped against her left breast sparking renewed arousal.

When he stepped into the dark kitchen, she wondered how he could see anything in the unfamiliar surroundings. Impulsively she reached up and splayed her hands across the tight band of his chest muscles, curling her fingers in the light mat of hair and holding tight just in case he fell over a chair or something.

Beneath her hands, his heart thumped just as wildly as hers did.

As he kicked the kitchen door closed, a breeze caught a tangle of his hair, blowing it over his forehead giving him a terribly sexy appeal she just couldn't resist. Lifting her head, she kissed him full on the mouth.

She tasted her cum on his lips. She'd never tasted it before. It was rather sweet and spicy, an interesting flavor.

He kissed her back eagerly, an untamed promise of delicious things to come. His tongue prodded deep into her mouth making her world tilt with pleasure.

She hadn't even realized they were in her bedroom until cool sheets melted beneath her backside as he deposited her on her bed.

"Where's your pantyhose?" he whispered when he broke the kiss.

"My pantyhose?"

"Where do you keep them?"

"Why?"

"So I can tie you down and fuck you senseless."

Oh, my gosh!

Being tied down while a man made love to her had always been one of her fantasies and now that she was coming face to face with it, she hesitated.

She didn't even know this guy!

They'd only done oral sex on each other and now he was asking her to trust him by having him tie her down? To her surprise, the idea of a stranger taking her in such an intimate trusting way just about made her orgasm on the spot.

She couldn't stop the giggle from escaping her lips at the insanity of it.

Of wanting this man to fuck her for as long and as hard as he wanted while she lay on the bed totally helpless to stop him.

Besides, she shouldn't be afraid, he'd cleared security. His references were good. He was a handyman. A ship mechanic. He'd worked for friends of hers. Her security team had sent him to her yacht. They knew he was here. He wouldn't try to would harm her.

"If you rather I don't..." his eyes sparkled down at her with a hope she couldn't resist.

"Top left drawer. And hurry!"

He hurried and found what he needed.

The sexy way his muscles played across his big chest and arms as he tied her wrists ignited a wild fire deep inside her pussy.

Within a minute, he had her arms tied to her bedposts. He left her legs free.

He leaned over her. Kissing her neck, his lips left a trail of wet fire as he teasingly moved over the swells of her breasts, along the rounded curve of her belly, circling her quivering clit like a vulture until she writhed helplessly on the bed.

When he stood, he flicked on a nearby light switch bathing them both with a warm buttery glow.

Jade's heart crashed against her chest like a jackhammer as he dropped his pants and climbed out of his underwear.

He straightened and Jade gulped at his awesome erection.

Outside in the moonlit darkness when she'd taken him orally she'd seen what a lovely size of a cock he possessed, but now here in her cozy bedroom with the pine paneled walls and dainty white curtains flowing behind him, she could see his magnificent pulsing size was a heck of a lot bigger than she'd thought.

The mushroom-shaped head looked red and fierce.

Ready to impale her.

Her pussy quivered in anticipation.

Have mercy but the man was extremely well hung.

Large cock.

Nice manners.

Good-looking.

Sexy.

Everything she'd ever dreamed about her man being.

A nice fluttering feeling zipped through her lower belly. Her face flushed at the thought that this man could be the one.

"You're blushing," he smiled.

"I've never...never seen such a big cock before," she said truthfully.

His white teeth flashed as he grinned.

"Before long I'll have your whole body blushing, Jade. Spread your legs for me."

She swallowed her excitement and did as he instructed.

This time it was his turn to exhale softly.

"Your clit is beautiful and puffy. Your pussy, soaking wet. Just the way I like it. Just the way I need you. You did good, keeping yourself aroused, Jade. You're almost ready for me. First, I have to prepare you. I'll be back in a minute."

Before she could ask him where he was going, he'd vanished.

A couple of minutes later, he returned holding the bowl of raw vegetables in his hand.

"I saw the way you looked at them during dinner. It gave me some delicious ideas."

"What kind of ideas?" she could barely speak from all the excitement washing over her senses.

He grinned wickedly. "You'll see."

Instincts told her this man was going to do something naughty to her with those vegetables.

Something wicked.

God help her she wanted him to do all sorts of things to her body.

Her senses exploded when he pulled a long thick carrot from the bowl.

Long male fingers stroked the orange object in the same tender way he'd done to it earlier after dinner. The carrot was about half the width of Caydon's cock and about half as long.

"Vegetables are called the poor man's sex toys, Jade. We'll have to use these until I can get us some proper ones."

Poor man's sex toys? Until he can get proper toys?

Exactly how long did he plan on staying? How long did he plan on having her tied up here?

The questions sat at the tip of her tongue but she didn't dare ask. To tell the truth she didn't want to know when he planned on leaving her. For now, she just wanted to pretend this man was hers, forever.

"Time to see how much you can take, Jade."

"I can take whatever you dish out, Minnelli," she threw back.

He inhaled sharply at her trembling words. His eyes darkened in the same way they'd done when he'd instructed her to pinch and pull at her nipples until the pleasure-pain had become so unbearable she'd cried out.

"We'll see how much you can take, Jade. Spread your legs wider for me, honey. I'm going to give you something you won't soon forget."

Moisture dripped from her pussy at the husky promise in his voice. The scorching look in his eyes turned her into a slab of heat and her pussy into a quivering mess. Even her breasts reacted to his intense gaze by tightening, swelling, becoming hard and eager to be caressed.

He leaned over her, the warm head of his rigid cock poked deliciously into her belly button as he grabbed a nearby pillow. Fluffing it up he stuffed it beneath her hips, which allowed him to raise her up higher exposing her fully to him.

"There, that's much more comfortable. This will give me the perfect angle to enter you."

Jade swallowed a whimper of arousal.

She could barely breathe as she watched him guide the big, thick carrot between her legs.

When she felt the smooth rounded end of the vegetable rubbing gently at her clit, she sucked in a heated breath.

"I'll just get you back into the mood," he whispered.

"I'm already in the mood."

"Vegetables turn you on, do they?"

"Along with the man holding them," she admitted.

"I'm glad you approve of my abilities to arouse."

"That's an understatement," she breathed. "You're like magic when you touch me."

The sensual way the head of the carrot stroked her quivering clit was making her come alive with delicious sensations.

Her legs fell further apart.

Her pussy hummed. Her heart sang at the intense way he was looking at the area between her legs, the concentration twisting his lips while he worked her clitoris.

"Magical fingers can earn a man a decent living. A magical cock can earn a man a woman's love for life."

Jade swallowed at the sound of his husky voice.

Some lucky woman would have this gorgeous man and his throbbing cock one day. Oh! How she hoped what she'd wished on that falling star tonight would come true.

It had been a silly wish though. A wish about a man she knew nothing about.

But what he'd done to her and was doing was a good start.

She watched his eyes slowly glaze. She felt her velvety folds of her labia part and he slid the thick item into her channel. Her vaginal muscles clenched tightly around the foreign object and she cried out at the delicious tremors as it stretched her.

"You're nice and tight, Jade. Tight and wet."

Her hips moved in little thrusts and her body trembled as he slid the carrot in and out between the swollen tissues of her heated vagina.

"Harder?" he asked as she clenched her teeth and fought for release.

She nodded, totally transfixed by the wonderful way the muscles in his arms rippled as he pulled back and thrust the carrot into her pussy nice and hard. It surged deep into her, but not filling her to completion.

Giggling, she suddenly realized the carrot was about the same size as her ex, Beau.

Caydon grinned with curiosity. "What's so funny?"

"It's too small."

"Too small, huh? Well, we'll have to take care of that problem, won't we?"

Pulling the carrot back, it popped out with a big slurpy sound. Placing it into the bowl, he took out the slender English style cucumber and stroked it the same sensual way he'd done to the carrot.

My goodness! The cucumber looked almost twice as long as the carrot and twice as thick. But still not as big as Caydon's fierce-looking cock.

She held her breath as he directed the green item between her legs. It felt cool as he nudged it inside.

Slurpy sounds split the air as her pussy embraced the vegetable.

He sank it into her slowly, cautiously.

At the same time, his finger toyed with her sensitive clit, igniting a flame.

She closed her eyes and moaned at the pleasurable sensations. He began in slow easy strokes, fucking into her eager pussy, dragging the vegetable out then probing deeper with each entry.

Pulling out the cucumber again, he impaled her with one delicious thrust that threw her to the edge of a climax. Instinctively, she arched her hips higher wanting a deeper penetration, but groaned in frustration when he whispered, "I'm in all the way to the hilt, sweetie."

"You're a tease, Minnelli," she gasped trying hard to control her breathing.

She sobbed and tried hard not to yell and scream and demand him to satisfy her, this instant.

"So, you're looking for some heavier action, are you?"

"I want your cock, Caydon."

"You're that confident I'll fit, are you?" he breathed.

Her eyes snapped open and she read the uncertainty on his face.

Jade swallowed and suddenly realized why he was playing this game with the vegetables. He wanted to make sure he would fit her.

"I need a big man to fill the ache deep inside me. I've always craved one," she said truthfully.

She heard him groan in response, yet the uncertainty remained in his gaze.

"I don't want to hurt you, Jade."

Frustration clawed at her and her patience waned. She yanked on her binds.

"I want you to fuck me, as hard as you can. I want to feel you deep inside me. I need it. I need you so bad."

Excitement exploded in his eyes. Perspiration sheened his forehead, oiled his lovely muscular chest.

"I'm going to make love to you like you've never been made love to before, Jade Hart."

Shivering with anticipation, she watched as he stalked to the end of the bed. Watched him saunter as if he were an animal in heat ready to claim his mate. Her blood pumped furiously through her veins in anticipation of being impaled with his rock-hard cock. Her breaths were heavy and labored, pushing her swollen breasts high. Her nipples felt puffy and stiff. Ready to be claimed by his masculine chest.

She widened her legs further and angled her hips upward giving him a great view of what awaited him.

Masculine muscles burst in his biceps as with hands and knees he climbed onto the bed between her legs.

Jade's heart crashed furiously against her chest as he came over her like a god. His naked body oiled by perspiration. His eyes glazed with lust. His wonderful cock hung like a molten piece of steel and to her delight, it was aimed straight at her pussy. In the shadows of his pubic hair beneath his engorged cock, she saw his balls nestled heavy and full, ready to burst.

Hot arms scalded against the sensitive side curves of her breasts, his hands came down tangling in the sheets beside her and his body descended upon hers with the tenderness of a soft downy blanket.

Powerful masculine legs aligned themselves on top of hers, his feet cradled side by side with hers.

She inhaled sharply as his huge cock sliced apart her drenched labia lips and he poised his heavy swollen flesh at the door of her wet pussy.

"Are you sure you want this? Do you want me to make love to you?" His breath brushed across her bangs and caressed her face.

Jade hesitated.

God! How could she be sure about anything?

It was all happening too fast.

Mere days ago she'd filled out a Kidnap Fantasies questionnaire asking for a well-hung man.

The biggest cock in stock, she'd written.

She'd never mailed the questionnaire in. Yet, here was exactly what she'd ordered.

A thick penis. So hard looking, so purple with arousal that she could barely contain the frustration at wanting him to slam into her over and over again.

And yet, he was so big.

Bigger than anything she'd created in her fantasies.

So wonderfully, blessedly huge.

Her pussy quivered with a need so immense she couldn't stop herself from whimpering every time she looked at his piece of raw pulsing flesh.

Oh yes! She wanted his shaft to satisfy that throbbing ache deep inside her womb.

But would his size hurt her?

She was willing to take that chance.

"I'm sure," she could barely speak now. Her body felt so tight, so ready for him she could just scream.

Caydon's nostrils flared in arousal. His eyes smoldered a deep lusty blue.

"You're so beautiful, sweetie. So damn beautiful. If only I'd known sooner..."

Before she had a chance to ask what he meant he rolled a bit to the side and using one arm to keep himself from coming fully down on top of her he lifted his other hand off the bed and it slipped between them settling his hot palm onto her stomach.

Such a huge palm.

A very gentle palm that slid warmly over her abdomen, through the tangle of the crisp curls covering her mons. She cried out her pleasure the instant he touched her clit where he began to work his magic with his fingers.

While he massaged, he sank his cock into her.

Slowly. Ever so agonizingly slow.

His large size pushed against her snug passage. Her vaginal muscles spasmed, contracted, and gripped him.

He groaned.

It was a guttural sound as if he were in pain. But it was a beautiful sound too and it sent shivers up and down her arms.

"What did you wish for on that star?" he said hotly as his heat-seeking cock split her wide open.

"What?" Jade could barely keep her eyes open. Could hardly breathe. Could barely stem the quickly rising orgasm as his finger continued to slide over her sensitized clitoris.

"The falling star," he ground out between clenched teeth. "What did you wish for?"

"I'm...not...telling."

She sank into the pleasure taking hold. Her vaginal muscles quivered as he drove his cock deeper into her. He stretched her like she'd never been stretched before.

"Is this what you wished for? To get fucked by me?"

She tossed her head back and forth suddenly unable to speak.

"What does that mean? No? You didn't wish for me to fuck you? Or no, you aren't going to tell me?"

God! Why was he questioning her like this?

"No... I didn't wish for...this...," she groaned as his cock slid against sensitive spots. "It...sure comes...a close...second."

He grinned and shifted his hips slightly to allow for a deeper penetration.

Jade gasped at the sparkle of pleasure-pain zipping inside her channel.

He pushed his steely shaft deeper.

"Tell me your wish," he whispered as his lips sipped on the bottom curves of her mouth.

"Uh...uh not until it...comes true."

"Ah, there's confidence in that statement. Does it have something to do with me?"

A fantastic burst of pleasure zipped up her vagina as he pressed harder on her clitoris.

"Oh God!" she gasped and pulled frantically at her pantyhose restraints wanting desperately to curl her arms around his neck and pull him into a kiss.

He chuckled against her mouth.

"I love seeing you like this, sweetie. Love feeling the way your hips arch into me, the way your hot channel feels as its velvety sides grabs hold of me and sucks me in. I want to fuck you so hard that you won't be able to escape me because you'll be too exhausted from all those orgasms I'm going to give you."

His mouth came down upon hers with such passion it took the breath clean out of her lungs.

His lips moved overs hers with strong and powerful kisses. His five o'clock shadow brushed erotically against her flesh. He kissed her so slowly and so deeply, she became disoriented. If anyone asked her her name, she wouldn't have been able to tell them. Her mind was mush. As for the heavenly sensations claiming her body...she loved it.

She barely realized he'd withdrawn until she heard a suctioning sound as he left her. Then he reentered in one smooth hard thrust. With each stroke of his cock, her sexual tension mounted.

Several times, he broke the kisses, his mouth lingering on her lips as he whispered her name. She loved the softness of his voice and instinctively moved against him, her hips writhing beneath him as she lost self-control.

As he buried his hot length incredibly deep inside her, Jade finally came apart. Squeezing her eyes shut against the rich assault, she spiraled into killing pleasure.

He slid his thick cock in and out of her in long, deep, torturous strokes. Perspiration broke out on her flushed skin.

The smell of their sex swung past her nostrils.

His mouth bruised hers. His chest hairs sparked a blaze in her nipples. His rock-hard chest flattened her swollen breasts and his sexy throaty grunts encouraged her to meet his every thrust with frantic enthusiasm of her own.

She wrapped her legs around his hips, the soles of her feet digging into his firm ass cheeks allowing for an even deeper penetration.

His tongue plunged into her mouth repeatedly, matching the strong confident thrusts of his cock as he impaled her again and again until they were moaning and gasping within the pleasure.

He pumped harder.

Violent tremors snapped through her, blinding her with craving. His thick, long shaft was hard and unyielding. His touches sensual and caressing.

He wrapped her in a world of desire, of lusty torture and of exquisite satisfaction. She clutched at his back as she came over and over. He claimed her, made her weep and utterly drained her of her strength, molding her into a ball of wild lust.

She didn't know how long he fucked her, but her climaxes seemed endless. Luscious. Lovely.

Finally, he filled her with his hot cum. Thick jets spewed into her body. His cream claimed her vagina and branded her body with his sperm.

When he was finished, he withdrew and moved off her. The restraints fell away from her wrists.

She couldn't budge. Her pussy throbbed and spasmed from the after glow of sex. This was...wonderous. More than any fantasy she'd come up with.

Sweet exhaustion claimed her limbs. She was too weak from the fantastic fucking and all those exploding orgasms.

She was even too tired to open her eyes.

She gasped softly as he climbed onto her again, moaned as his semi-hard cock impaled her again. Raw pleasure-pain sifted along her channel as he buried his thick length right to the hilt. Then he rolled them onto their sides.

Instinctively she knew he was finished with her for the night. Knew that he wanted to lie this way with his thick gorgeous cock cradled safely inside her wet pussy.

He leaned his bristly cheek against her damp one. She sighed contentedly and nuzzled against him.

His breath flowed over her in delicious waves.

Before she fell asleep, she heard him whisper softly, "Tomorrow is another day."

She knew he meant he'd be making love to her again. And again. And again.

Chapter Five

Christmas Eve morning...

Déjà vu, Jade thought as she awoke to the delicious scent of coffee sifting through her tiny bedroom.

Yesterday he'd made her dinner. Today, would it be breakfast?

Gosh, what had she done to get so lucky?

Her happiness, however, was short-lived.

Why was he being so nice to her? Was he wheedling his way into her graces because she had money? Was Caydon like her ex?

No, please God, don't let him just be using me.

Okay, so maybe he might be using her. But she was using him too.

For great sex.

She was using him to fulfill some of her wildest fantasies and she didn't even have to tell him what they were. He already knew what she wanted.

He was perfect. Too perfect.

Again a niggle of uneasiness zipped up her spine. A man like Caydon could have any woman he wanted. Why pick her?

She was a virtual cripple. A millionaire invalid.

Jade sighed in frustration, closed her eyes and bit the curve of her lower lip. It felt bruised and sensitive from his fierce kisses.

Kisses she'd thoroughly enjoyed. Kisses she wouldn't mind experiencing for the rest of her life.

Stupid girl. You're getting yourself all tied up in knots over nothing! He didn't say he wanted to marry you. He didn't even say he was staying beyond today. God, you are such a loser dreaming such stupid dreams.

Besides, tomorrow was Christmas. Surely, he had some family waiting for him somewhere, despite his saying he didn't have to visit them this year.

A mother. Father.

Brothers? Sisters?

And he'd already said he wasn't married or had a girlfriend.

Besides, it was just casual hot sex between them. Her momentary boy toy. Something that had occurred naturally between a hot-blooded gorgeous American male and a semi-attractive woman who sunbathed partially nude.

She shouldn't even be worried about him being after her money. She hadn't even spent a red cent on the man. And he hadn't asked her to.

She was reading way too much into this. Unfortunately, since Beau dumped her she'd been jumping to conclusions about every single guy who'd even looked at her with interest.

Mutual sex was their only common interest.

With that thought planted firmly in her mind, she pushed the sheets aside and sucked in a breath at the wonderful ache sparkling the entire length of her pussy.

Whoa!

The guy sure had filled her vagina with that excruciatingly beautiful sized cock.

She could feel the rawness, the sweet hurt deep inside her.

Jade smiled.

The rawness should produce some exceptionally delicious sex the next time he penetrated her.

Gosh, she couldn't wait until they had sex again.

She scooted out of bed and to her surprise, her hip barely ached after all the fucking she'd experienced last night. To her further surprise, she found her cane settled right beside her bed. Her body filled with a warm happy glow. Bless that well-hung man's heart for thinking of bringing it to her.

Fifteen minutes later, Jade had showered and dressed in a flowing white cotton knee-length skirt, a dark pink T-shirt and a light pink, long-sleeved cotton shirt to kick off the early morning chill from the ocean fog.

Grabbing her cane, she limped along and followed the tantalizing trail of bacon and eggs to where she found Caydon slaving over a hot stove already fully dressed in the same sexy white shirt he'd worn yesterday and the same tight jeans that cupped a sensually shaped tush.

When he spied her standing in the doorway ogling his nice derriere, he grinned. Cute dimples burst wide open in his cheeks making Jade's breath back up all the way into her lungs.

"Hiya pretty lady, I've got flapjacks, bacon, eggs, toast is in the toaster and your coffee...straight black, is right here," he poured a cup of steaming black coffee for her and handed her the mug.

She accepted it with a grateful smile and eagerly took a sip of the hot liquid.

"It tastes wonderful. Thank you."

"Before we do anything else today I want you to wear these." He scooped something off a plate set on the counter. To her surprise he held up two, ping-pong sized balls that hung from a string.

"What are they?"

"Pleasure balls. They go inside you. Up your vagina."

Her cheeks heated up with excitement.

A sex toy? This guy is unbelievable!

"In each of these devices is a small rotating bearing. Every time you move they give off a vibrating sensation."

"Where'd you get them?"

"While you were sleeping I fixed the engines and berthed us here." He nodded toward the nearby window where to her shock she noticed through the rising mist the masts of sailboats and shadowy silhouettes of unfamiliar cruisers and yachts.

"Where are we?"

"A town south of Tampa Bay. They've got a great sex shop in a private home I know about not far from the mall. I've been here before so you don't need to play guide. Now back to the pleasure balls. I've already lubricated them. Would you allow me to do the honors?"

The honors? He wanted to put them inside her?

She nodded, her anticipation building. Gosh, she couldn't believe she was allowing a virtual stranger, a sexy hunk, to insert foreign objects into her vagina. She'd always considered herself shy yet this man was making her feel so at ease with his natural attitude toward sex she didn't even think about hesitating in doing what the handyman ordered.

"Drop your skirt and underwear and sink that pretty little ass of yours onto the table."

Despite her sudden newfound freedom, she couldn't stop her face from flushing with heat.

Her heart quickened, her blood grew hot in her veins and her vaginal muscles quivered.

He took her coffee mug and the cane from her and plopped them on the far side of the table.

An odd little noise sounded in his throat that made Jade smile as he watched her slip her skirt down her legs. She did the same with her panties gliding it off slowly and as sexy as she could.

Her breath felt heavy in her chest at the thought of him mounting her right here on the table. Wouldn't that be awesome if he did? Maybe she should ask him to do her. Maybe she should tease him into it.

Her pussy creamed at that thought.

She looked into his eyes, the dark color of denim. There was a ripe expression sparkling in there, a cheerfulness that made her heart leap with curiosity. He was a stranger but instinctively she knew he was up to something and it was something she was sure she would love.

She dropped her gaze. The heavenly bulge between his legs seemed to grow right before her eyes making a savage hunger ripple through her. She could barely stop herself from reaching out to yank down his zipper.

He was aroused.

Just as much as she was.

Obviously, he had better self-control than she did.

To her disappointment, he shook his head. "No time for fun right now, pretty lady. I've got plans for you."

Strong hands curled around her hips and he lifted her off the floor as if she were as light as a feather. She gasped as her ass hit the cool table.

Gosh, he smelled good this morning. His fresh male scent danced all around her. Combined with a hint of soap it was turning out to be the best smell in the world. It made her feel hotter than ever. Hoisting her feet onto the table she once again noticed the tightness that had lingered in her hip over the past year wasn't as bad anymore.

Maybe last night's ferocious fucking had loosened her up.

To her surprise, she could spread her legs wide without too much trouble and held her breath as he crouched down between her legs.

Excitement coursed through her veins as he smiled with approval.

"Pink, puffy and wet. Just the way I want you."

She exhaled as the large palm of his hand blazed a line of heat along her inner thighs until his fingers met her crotch area.

"The balls are lubricated with some jelly for easy insertion," his voice sounded strangled, his hot gaze fixed directly at her trembling pussy.

Her pussy muscles spasmed as he slid the pleasure ball between her throbbing labia lips and stuffed the first one up inside her tight wet channel. The second quickly followed.

"You're so perfectly tight I doubt I'll have to adjust it much during the day but maybe I'll have to make up excuses to check."

Oh sweet heavens!

"The string dangles so I can remove it when I want to fuck you."

Jade sucked in an aroused breath.

"Wiggle your hips for me," he instructed.

She did as he asked and sighed at the sultry sensations when the tiny erotic vibrations rippled inside her vagina.

"How's it feel?"

She couldn't stop her eager giggle. "Like I want to be fucked."

"Good, it'll keep you in a state of arousal while we shop."

Shop? The man wanted to shop when she wanted to be fucked? The only thing on her mind right now was to take him into her bedroom, or better yet writhe beneath him on this table, while he slid his yummy huge cock in and out of her just as he'd done last night.

"Shopping? Exactly what are we shopping for?"

His dark gaze met hers. Childish excitement flashed across his face.

"Christmas presents. I haven't finished shopping for presents. How about you?"

"Well...no," she lied.

She'd already given her two sisters their presents when they'd showed up unexpectedly but now that he mentioned Christmas shopping she wouldn't mind picking up a little something for him. A little thank you for last night.

"Great! We're going to shop till you drop." His warm hands sensuously cupped her naked hips as he hoisted her off the table and placed her feet firmly on the floor again.

"Don't put your underwear back on. Just the skirt. Are you wearing a bra?"

"No."

"Good, I have some surprises stored up for you today while we shop. Then we'll come back here and I'll fuck you till I drop."

Goodness, the man had a way with words.

She creamed, thankful that she wasn't wearing her underwear.

He released her hips and headed back to the stove.

"Breakfast is ready. Let's eat. The sooner we leave, the sooner we get back."

* * * * *

With each and every step the pleasure balls vibrated teasingly inside her vagina.

Thank goodness, she hadn't worn her panties. It would have been most uncomfortable plastered between her legs. As it was now she could feel her sticky juices sliding down the insides of her thighs.

They'd been here a little over three hours and the pleasure balls had made Jade so horny she was quite ready to head back to the boat to spend the rest of what was left of this day doing some good old hard fucking.

Yet, she still hadn't picked out a present for Caydon and she still had no idea what to get him. Whatever she picked though would have to be perfect.

Laughing and chattering with him as they moved from store to store, she'd been able to pry out some intimate details of his life.

Aside from his confession of loving to cook, she discovered he had a love for fishing. There were other things he'd dropped hints about. He enjoyed the outdoors, loved swimming and craved to learn how to ski downhill. She kept all these tidbits stored in her mind waiting until they decided to separate and buy gifts for each other...that is if he wanted to buy gifts for each other.

She hadn't had the nerve to ask him about that yet.

However, she found herself getting truly excited as she helped him pick out gifts for his mother, father and to her surprise, he even asked her to help him pick out some things for his two sisters and two brothers.

All his siblings were younger than him. None of them were currently married and they didn't have any kids.

"So you really think the tea set I picked out is okay for your grandmother?"

He'd dragged her into an expensive little china boutique where he'd asked her to choose the pattern for an elegant tea set.

She'd picked a fancy shaped white teapot patterned with delicate pink forget-me-nots with a matching set of twelve teacups, saucers and cake plates.

Caydon had nodded his appreciation.

When she'd looked at the price tag however she'd just about balked. Caydon was a handyman. He couldn't afford her expensive tastes.

To her shock, he didn't even flinch at the price. He'd drawn out his credit card, made the purchase and asked for it to be gift-wrapped.

They'd lugged all the presents to a post office where he sent them off via courier laughing when she told him the presents would never be delivered on time. Apparently, it was a tradition that his presents were always late.

"My grandmother would have picked out the same pattern," he said. "She loves flowers and she loves delicate designs. The teapot she has right now is literally falling apart. It must be more than fifty years old."

He curled his arm around her elbow, and hugged her close as they stepped into the crowded mall complete with screaming kids, cheerful Christmas music and the smell of popcorn sifting through the air from a nearby vendor.

"Gram was the same way. She kept everything. When my sisters and I inherited her things we were really glad she hadn't thrown stuff away because everything has a memory attached to it."

"Do you think that maybe I shouldn't have gotten her a teapot?" He looked worried.

"Oh, I didn't mean that you shouldn't have. Gram had three sets of them. One was for family. One for company and the other was for Sundays. Grandmothers can never have too many tea sets hanging around the house."

Relief washed over Caydon's face and he nodded in agreement. "She'll probably need a bunch of them for when her future grandkids come over and start breaking things."

Jade laughed. "My sister Johnna and her husband are expecting their first baby in about eight months."

He looked down at her, a play of emotions she couldn't describe flashed in his eyes. "How about you? Do you want any kids?"

She shrugged. "I never really thought too much about it. My skiing career was my main priority in my life but now that I think about it I wouldn't mind having one or two."

He nodded.

"I want a lot of them. Maybe five kids just like my mom and pop had."

Jade's eyes widened in shock.

"My God! Five kids!"

"It was kind of nice being the oldest and helping my parents with the younger ones. I know how to change diapers, do the required burping, the whole shebang. Any woman would be lucky to snag me. She'd have herself a live-in babysitter."

"With a brood of five you could play Santa Claus too."

She nodded to the middle of the mall where a rumpled-looking man dressed in a red and black Santa Claus suit, complete with a curly white beard, sat on a gray throne with a sad-looking castle behind him.

On both knees, he bounced two bawling twin toddlers while shouting out a happy "Ho! Ho! Ho!" Curled in his arms were two sleeping babies who were also identical twins. A harried-looking man, who Jade figured was the father, stood to the side with an empty double-stroller while the cheerful female elf, dressed in shiny green garb, quickly snapped pictures of the fiasco.

From beside her, Caydon chuckled. "The dad looks beat."

"He looks like he's ready to crash and burn."

They left the scene behind as he suddenly pulled her into another store.

To her surprise, it was a lingerie boutique complete with frilly teddies and sexy panties with openings in the most intimate places.

An older sales clerk quickly tracked them down.

"Merry Christmas!" she cooed. "May I help you?"

"We're looking for something really sexy for my honey bun," Cayden said and winked at the lady.

Honey bun? Oh my God! Get serious!

Jade flushed as the sales lady winked at her.

"Did you have anything particular in mind?" The woman asked Caydon who was already eyeing a very pretty white lace see-through teddiette.

"I love this one. Do you have one in a jade color?"

"Oh you have fantastic taste. This design just came in yesterday. Yes, we do have it in that color. And I have a size that will fit her perfectly."

"I'll take it."

"Caydon!" she complained.

What? he mouthed to her and then grinned and hugged her to him as he smiled at the woman.

"Oh honey buns, you'll look fabulous in it. Can she put it on in the change room?"

"Of course, sir."

Her heart cracked against her chest as the sales lady quickly shifted through the hangers and found a pretty jade-colored one. Caydon began humming a Christmas tune beside her and hugged her tighter as if not wanting her to run away.

Why did she suddenly get the feeling he was up to something naughty?

"The teddiette has a Lycra back, underwire bra, adjustable garters, snap bottom—"

"It looks perfect." Caydon snapped the sexy piece of lingerie from the sales lady and quickly handed it to Jade.

"Go on in and put it on, honey buns."

Jade cleared her throat at the scorching look blazing his eyes.

Sweet sunshine! If looks could fuck, he'd be doing her right now.

She nodded shakily and headed toward a secluded back door that said Fitting Rooms.

The area appeared to be empty and she headed to the far-end stall. Once inside, she quickly stripped and put the sexy little outfit on.

Turning around she admired it in the mirror.

The sales person was right. The man definitely had great taste. The see-through lace hugged her every curve, outlining her breasts and allowing her peaked nipples to poke seductively against the soft fabric.

To her surprise, the rest of it fit as if it were a second skin.

There was a quick knock at the door and to her horror, Caydon stepped inside and closed the door behind him.

"Wow, you look hot enough to fuck right here and now," he whispered. "And you look downright horny."

"You're not supposed to be in here!" she whispered.

"Why not?" he chuckled. "I gave her a twenty to let me in."

"You didn't!"

"I did," he said proudly.

She resisted the overwhelming urge to throw her arms around his neck and start kissing him right then and there, or yank his gorgeous cock out of his jeans and guide it right into her hot and waiting pussy.

As if reading her thoughts he said softly, "That's the way I like my woman. Hot and horny for me. Those pleasure balls are working I take it?"

"You have to ask?"

He pushed her against the wall, and boxed her in with his large sinewy arms. His eyes blazed as he lowered his head and brushed his lips against hers in a smooth feather light touch that made her senses riot.

"I have to feel you," he said huskily.

"What? Here? Now?"

"You sound properly shocked. How about I shock you some more?"

His large hand cupped her soaked pussy.

She tightened. Blood quickened in her veins.

God! She wanted to be fucked right now!

Reaching out, she flattened her hands against the muscular expanse of his solid chest and arched her pussy really hard into his palm in a desperate attempt to grind herself into a climax. He quickly found the snaps and the material that had been the teddiette's panties fell away. Cool air brushed against her wet pussy but it did nothing to douse her fevered heat.

Two masculine fingers plunged inside her drenched vagina. They felt like two wonderful blades of lightning and she gasped at the invasion.

"The pleasure balls have slipped down a bit, I'll adjust them."

"Caydon, I don't think..."

She wanted to say she didn't think this was a good place for him to be fingering her because she just might scream out her arousal but his mouth clamped over hers stopping her words dead in their tracks.

His lips were tantalizing, teasing and oh so yummy and she couldn't halt the tortured moan in her throat. Her eyes closed against the shivers as his fingers adjusted the pleasure balls pushing them higher into her vagina.

She weakened when his thumb rubbed erotically against her clit. Her pussy clenched in agonizing explosions and he kept his mouth sliding against hers, capturing her moans.

When the orgasm faded, he tore his mouth from hers and whispered huskily, "That's just a prelude of things to come."

Without warning, he unclasped the teddiette's underwire bra allowing her breasts to spill free.

He took her swollen globes into his hands, his thumbs harshly caressing her nipples.

She closed her eyes, threw her head back and gasped at the erotic stirrings snapping through her breasts. Her nipples swelled and hardened as he drew them out and plumped them. He spent a good couple of minutes with each sensitized nipple until her pussy quivered once again.

"Keep your eyes closed, my sweetness," he whispered.

Before she could ask why she felt an unusual tug on her left nipple. The tug tightened a little and then a second later she felt a similar tug and tightening on her right one.

Jade quaked with desire.

"What are you up to?" she breathed.

She wanted to open her eyes but didn't want to at the same time.

To her frustration, he moved away.

"Open your eyes, now."

Jade did as he asked and looked down.

Oh, my!

Her areolas, usually a hot pink had been turned to a pretty shade of knotted purple. And her nipples were a similar color. They were plump, stretched out and squeezed erotically between small nipple clamps.

Jade turned to look in the mirror.

Dangling from the nipple clamps were thin one-inch silver chains and at the end of each chain sparkled a tiny pink diamond, or at least what looked to be diamonds.

She highly doubted they were real.

Another tiny chain linked her two nipples by drooping between the valley of her exposed breasts down to her belly button.

"You like?" he asked softly as he pushed his male body against her naked back. She didn't miss the massive bulge pressed intimately against the crack in her butt and suddenly she wanted him plunging into her from behind.

"Keep the teddiette and clamps on."

"Caydon..."

"Shh, the nipple clamps are safe. You can wear them for hours. You'll love it. I promise there's more to come."

Her head whirled. "More?"

He nodded. "Meet me in two hours at the restaurant around the corner. We're under the reservation of Minnelli."

Without waiting for an answer, he slipped out of the dressing room closing the door behind him.

Jade looked back at herself and exhaled a shaky aroused breath.

Her hair was a tangled mess.

Her cheeks were flushed a healthy pink as if she'd just been skiing all day in the mountains, her lips were swollen and red from his kisses and the tiny nipple clamps looked so erotic it just about drove her insane.

Now more than ever, she couldn't wait until they got back to her boat.

Jade grinned to herself.

It was her turn to pay Caydon back and she knew just how to do it.

* * * * *

The surprised look on Jade's face when she'd first looked down at her breasts and seen those clamps had turned Caydon's cock into a roaring serpent demanding immediate satisfaction.

By God, he'd wanted to take her right then and there in that dressing room. Wanted to thrust his cock deep into her delicious pussy until everyone heard her mewl in pleasure.

He'd almost done it too if he hadn't already mapped out the things he wanted to do to her for the rest of the day.

"Will that be everything, sir?" The elderly salesman asked.

"Yes, that's great."

"Where would you like all this delivered?"

Caydon gave him the address of the marina where he'd docked Jade's yacht and the name of the boat.

"If you could just set it on the foredeck out of sight and I'll take care of the rest."

"This must be your first Christmas with the wife," the older man chuckled.

"Wife?"

The old man chuckled louder.

"I saw both of you earlier when you strolled by arm in arm. You were looking at Santa Claus. You're a very striking couple. I couldn't help but notice she was limping with a cane. She must have been in an accident. She looks familiar. Is she a model or something?"

"Or something," Caydon winked.

He didn't want to tell the salesman Jade had been a famous downhill skier or that she'd been on the front cover of every gossip rag in the United States a few days ago with her cute breasts blurred out making it quite obvious she'd been sunbathing topless.

"Mrs. Minnelli will be quite surprised, sir. Thank you very much for your business, sir." The elderly man handed Caydon back his credit card. "The delivery will be there within the hour."

"Thank you!"

A little beeping sound emitted from Caydon's watch startling him.

"I better get a move on. Meeting the wife for an early supper. Thanks again."

The salesman threw Caydon a wave as he slipped out of the store and back into the mall.

Suddenly he couldn't wait to get back to Jade and to the next surprise he had in store for her.

Chapter Six

The restaurant Caydon had mentioned was beautifully decked out in seasonal garb. Green garland splashed with sprays of red rosehips intertwined with blinking gold lights were draped along the walls of the secluded booth the waitress had given her when Jade had told her she had reservations under the name Minnelli.

Romantic Christmas songs played softly in the background and the table had a traditional red and green theme giving the booth a cheerful and bright appearance.

The tablecloth was plain red cotton, the wineglasses were ruby-colored and the napkins were a charming forest green, the edges lined with red thread.

Jade laughed at the cute Santa Claus napkin rings and admired the gorgeous sphere-shaped Santa Claus ornaments set at the top of each place setting.

Stainless steel cutlery and silver plates sparkled in front of her and she realized not only was she starving for sex, she was hungry for food as well.

As she allowed her gaze to wander out of the booth, she noted that there were no other tables visible from where she sat. But she was allowed a luxurious view of a tiny stone pond nestled in the nearby corner. It came complete with running water, floating lily pads and gold-sprayed wheat cone trees nestled in miniature French iron bathtubs that hugged wild foliage at the edges of the miniature pond.

Her heart scrambled into a mad pace, the instant she heard the distinct voice of Caydon speaking to someone nearby. She couldn't make out his words but when she peeked out of the secluded booth she spotted him conversing with a waitress.

The muscles in her pussy clenched tightly at the sight of him. Her breath backed up into her lungs and desire stabbed her body.

His jeans and white shirt were gone replaced by a pair of dark blue slacks and a gray shirt that stretched across his wide well muscled chest.

And he'd gotten a haircut and a shave.

Gosh, he seemed even more handsome now than two hours ago and hunkier than yesterday when she'd first met him.

Jade shook her head in puzzlement.

Yesterday morning her life had been so ho-hum. Today she was looking forward to spending the rest of her life getting fucked by this perfect male specimen with the nice juicy big cock.

The rest of her life! And she didn't even know him!

Rein yourself in girl. You're getting ahead of yourself again. It's just a sexual relationship. Don't be so naive. Nothing will come of it. Just enjoy the sex while you can.

She studied him as he laughed easily with the waitress. She noted the confident way he stood. Loved the snug way his pants cupped his full ass. Most of all she loved the charming way he nodded his head in agreement with whatever the waitress was now saying to him.

His luscious lips were upturned into that sexy smile that made Jade's toes curl with excitement. But those cute dimples weren't playing along his cheeks like they did when he looked at her.

Oh pooh! She was reading too much into this guy again.

It seemed to be a very bad habit in getting her hopes up with this guy. She hoped she could break it once he decided it was time to leave her. Until that happened she was going to make the most of this man's company.

The breath stilled in her lungs when he turned and headed toward their booth.

Jade stuck her head back inside and waited for him.

"I missed you like crazy," he whispered as he slid onto the padded booth seat right beside her.

A delicious aroma of spicy aftershave washed over her senses making her dizzy with desire.

"I missed you too," she admitted truthfully. "A very nice haircut. Special occasion?"

His eyes roved to where her tight breasts were pushed up against the teddiette she wore beneath her T-shirt and shirt.

"A very special occasion. Those clamps still on?"

"Yes," Jade whispered as her blood boiled at his question.

She'd panicked in the fitting room as she'd redressed and seen the distinct outline of the clamps. Thankfully, when she'd put her loose shirt on top, the outline had diminished to something she thought she could handle.

A hint of a smile teased his lips. "Are they comfortable enough?"

"They're driving me crazy if you want to know the truth. My nipples are on fire. My pussy is sopping wet and I want relief."

He grinned, obviously happy with her sexual torture.

"And the pleasure balls?"

"They are waiting for your cock to replace them."

His eyes widened at her bold reply. "All in good time, Jade. All in good time. First though, I have another surprise for you."

"Dare I ask?"

Her heart cracked like a piston as he moved even closer to her, the entire side of his blistering body pressing intimately against hers. Hot masculine breath fanned her neck as he kissed her there and whispered, "Spread your legs."

Her eyes widened in surprise.

Quickly she glanced past him to make sure no one was watching and once again realized exactly how secluded this booth really was.

Her pussy creamed as she opened her legs wide beneath their dining table.

"I'm glad you wore a skirt today," he chuckled as his fingers burned against the inside of her knee.

"So am I."

"Wider," he whispered.

She did as he said and she just about bolted out of the chair when his scorching touch trailed along the inside of her upper thigh toward her clit.

When he reached it, he immediately sought her plump labia.

"You kept the teddiette underwear off?"

"It's in my purse, soaked."

He beamed happily obviously pleased with the thought she was creaming for him even after he'd left the dressing room.

Jade bit back a gasp as he pulled and twisted tenderly on her flesh until they burned delightfully. Then he drew her labia apart making them sting with a pleasure-pain that brought tears to her eyes.

"Did you do anymore shopping while we were apart?" he whispered into her ear.

"Yes and I've got a surprise for you. Call it..." she inhaled a breath as he affixed something slightly heavy to one side of her labia.

A clamp?

Her pussy lip throbbed.

She spread her thighs wider allowing him easier access.

"Call it payback for what you're doing to me now," she whispered.

"I like the sound of that."

He attached another clamp to the same side, just a little further up. This one so close to her sensitized pleasure nub she had to hold onto the sides of the table to keep herself from reaching between her legs and rubbing herself into a climax.

He fondled her other labia until Jade felt it swell, then he attached two clamps to it too. They gripped her flesh firmly holding her pussy in a charming form of sexual bondage she found appealing.

His fingers slid ever so gently between her tortured labia and he began a slow seductive massage against her clit.

Moaning softly at the sensual sensations, she eagerly waited for him to lead her into another climax like he'd done in the dressing room.

His warm cheek brushed erotically against the arc of her neck as he buried his face there again, this time nibbling on her ear sending ripples of delight shimmering through her.

"I would very much like to know what you have planned for me," his warm lips curved in a smile against her skin. "Perhaps I should masturbate you in order to get you to tell me."

She shivered. "You wouldn't dare."

Oh, please dare!

"I can tell by the glaze in your eyes, you'd love for me to do you right here."

His own eyes sparkled wonderfully.

"The waitress..."

"Don't worry about the waitress. She's busy getting our order."

Suddenly her clamped labia began to tingle.

"Caydon, what are you doing down there?"

He held up a small black remote box with a dial on it.

"Vibrating clamps. You like?"

"It's...different."

"Do they hurt?" he asked.

"They tingle."

"They've got little weights on them too."

"I feel them."

Gosh! Did she feel them!

"With the same style of pink diamond drops like those on your nipple clamps."

"Not real diamonds, I hope," she joked.

"That's for me to know and you to find out. Are you glad you aren't wearing underwear? Might have been a little too much pressure. You can wear these clamps for hours without any trouble."

Hours with these pleasing sensations rippling down there?

"I don't think I can wait that long, Caydon."

"Getting horny again?"

"More like still am."

"Sir? Ma'am? Your order is here."

Jade's face flamed as she looked up to see the waitress Caydon had been talking to only moments ago standing right outside their booth with a cart overflowing with food.

"You work fast around here," Caydon chuckled.

Thankfully, he slipped the remote box out of sight and into his pocket. He leaned closer against Jade, presumably so the waitress couldn't see he had a hand beneath the table and between her legs.

To her shock, she felt his finger continue to slide erotically against her pleasure nub as if they hadn't just been interrupted.

Bastard!

Jade's hands tightened on the table.

"Newlyweds?" The waitress grinned.

"Not yet." Caydon replied as he increased the pressure on Jade's clit.

Son of a bitch! Lady, get out of here!

"Nice day outside, isn't it?" The waitress poured some water into their glasses. "They're calling for it to be beautiful all the way through the rest of the year. We'll have a very sunny and warm Christmas and Happy New Year."

It's always beautiful weather in Florida! Get out of here before I orgasm right in front of you!

Jade gritted her teeth as she quickly slid toward the pleasure awaiting her.

Obviously thinking they were very much in love, the waitress smiled sweetly at both of them and quickly placed the covered plates onto the table along with a pitcher of what Jade perceived as eggnog.

"Would you like me to pour?"

No! Get out of here!

The waitress' face blurred and Jade felt her body stiffening from the arousal.

"No, thank you, that'll be fine." Caydon's voice was so calm she felt like crashing her fists against his chest.

The waitress took her cue and quickly left.

"Caydon!" Jade whimpered a warning.

The pressure from his finger increased and Jade slid over the edge. The instant the wild explosion cascaded through her body his sweet lips swooped down over hers capturing her quiet moans.

Dinner was both torture and wonderful.

Her beaded nipples ached with arousal beneath the nipple clamps. The labial vibrating clamps kept her squirming in her chair. Several times, she tried to press her legs together to bring herself off but the clamps bit painfully into her flesh. Obviously, the manufacturer had taken that into consideration when they'd designed the naughty toys.

If she didn't already have her revenge mapped out in her head she would have insisted he take her to the bathroom and drive his gorgeous cock deep into her dripping pussy.

It seemed as if there was no end to the food.

Caydon had ordered maple-glazed turkey for them, complete with mashed potatoes, peas and baby spinach.

During dinner they chatted about their likes and dislikes. When the server brought them their dessert, a scrumptious Berry Almond Trifle that arrived in a straight-sided clear glass trifle bowl that showed the irresistible palate pleasing layers of juicy red strawberries and plump blueberries, amaretto-soaked angel food cake and lip-smacking vanilla custard sprinkled with almonds, he prodded her about her childhood, and how she got into skiing professionally.

"Well, my parents got us all into skiing," she confessed. "From as early as I can remember every winter we had skis strapped to our feet. Even after my parents died in an avalanche and we moved in with Gram and Gramps, I couldn't stay off the slopes. I loved the sharp sting of snowflakes on my face, the sound of wind shrieking past my ears and the adrenalin rush flowing through my veins as I raced at speeds over a hundred kilometers down the mountainside. I felt so alive. So in tune with nature. And then..."

"And then came the crash."

She nodded.

"You sound as if you'll never feel alive again. As if you'll never strap a pair of skis on."

"I will someday...but they say I can never ski professionally again. But I'm one of those people who doesn't believe in never, so I am confident I will. Before I do ski again there's something else I want to do."

"Such as?"

"Sail to Europe. It's always been a dream of mine. Now that I have the time I can do it."

She'd expected him to laugh at her dream. He didn't.

Instead, he frowned with concern. "All by yourself?"

Was he looking for an invitation? Did she want to ask him? Could she ask him? Her brain told her she didn't even know the guy. They were good in the sack but she really didn't know if she could have him around her for months.

Her heart told her they could get along wherever they went.

She decided to listen to her brain. The last time she'd listened to her heart she'd been betrayed by a man.

Sadness tugged at her.

No, she wouldn't ask him. He wasn't in her plans. Heck, she didn't even know what her plans were about the future, hence the idea for the ocean trip.

"That's the plan."

"Are you sure it's safe?" Concern etched his words. "I mean a woman alone in the ocean. Things could happen. Storms. Engine problems. You could get sick. You should hire a competent crew. At least then if you run into trouble..."

"I want to be alone. I need time to think about things." Like to think about what she really wanted to do with the rest of her life. Maybe she really didn't want to get back into professional skiing anyways. Not that she was afraid. She wasn't. She just wanted to try new things.

He nodded. "I understand. You're going on a quest. You are a brave woman and a very sexy woman and I want to take you back to the boat and have my way with you. Are you up to that?"

"I thought you'd never ask."

* * * * *

"Oh my gosh. Caydon what have you done?"

Jade said as she clasped a hand over her mouth in wonder.

Through the soft glow of evening dusk, she spotted the row of champagne glasses, each filled with clear glass pebbles and each containing a flickering white votive candle, strewn along the mantel of what appeared to be a fireplace.

A fireplace, that sat smack in the middle of her yacht's deck.

"It's an electric fireplace. To set the mood," Caydon whispered as he helped her up the gangplank onto her boat.

"It looks so real. Even the flames look real."

She noted the two empty red Christmas stockings hanging near each end of the garland-dressed mantel.

Tears stung Jade's eyes as she stared at the flickering fireplace and then at the twinkling white miniature lights strung along the railings.

He'd made it look just like Christmas. All they needed now was a log cabin, fluffy snowflakes and a Christmas tree.

She shook her head in wonder. No guy had gone to so much trouble to do anything like this for her before. It seemed so...overwhelming.

She bit her bottom lip to keep herself from crying.

His warm hand touched her elbow.

"Are you okay? I didn't mean to make you cry."

Jade forced herself to smile and nodded, finding it hard to bite back the tears.

"Pop a couple of those chaise mattresses down in front of the fireplace and I'll be back in a few minutes."

When he disappeared into her yacht, the rush of tears burned the back of her eyes again and she rubbed them away with her fists.

The pretty flicker of orange flames in the fireplace drew her attention. She thought about all those evenings she'd spent in front of a real fire with Beau in hotel rooms all over the world. The heat from the flames had blasted against them while he'd drilled into her the next day's ski moves. He'd always been business first, pleasure second...if pleasure is what she could have called it back then.

Gosh, she'd been so immature regarding sex and men but now she knew better.

Maybe her skiing accident in Cortina had been a blessing in disguise.

As she'd lain in the hospital bed, her pain numbed with morphine, her hip stitched up after surgery and her leg plastered in a cast with the Italian doctor telling her in broken English she would never ski professionally again, Beau hadn't said a word. When she'd started to cry at the loss of her dream, he hadn't wrapped his arms around her in comfort. He'd simply shaken his head and walked out.

A few days later, she'd seen him on television announcing his new job coaching another professional downhill skier.

And that they were engaged, and she was pregnant with his child.

Son of a bitch!

Thank God, she'd met Caydon. He was a total opposite of Beau.

In bed and out. It was amazing how she'd responded to him and she'd loved all his surprises today and now this romantic fireplace...

Could Caydon Minnelli be the man in her future?

Jade shook the disturbing thoughts away. She needed to stay in reality. It meant this guy was just a fascinating fling who would get tired of her soon enough. In the meantime, she would enjoy all his attentions and the sizzling sex.

The clamps on her labia suddenly vibrated to life and Jade gasped at the sensual sensations it created.

Oh, the little bugger!

She'd give him his payback!

During the two hours they'd been separated she'd made a few purchases of her own and had them delivered to her boat asking them to specifically hide the goodies under the tarp in the bow.

Casting a quick glance over her shoulder to make sure Caydon wasn't around, she quickly headed to the bow area. Peeking under the tarp, she smiled at the shopping bags they'd delivered just as she'd asked. Caydon Minnelli was going to get his payback soon enough, but first she needed sexual satisfaction.

Quickly she returned to the deck where she threw down some lounge cushions in front of the fireplace and gingerly sat down careful not to disturb the aching labia clamps or wonderful burning nipple clamps.

Caydon showed up a moment later.

"Here, I whipped you up some sparkling cranberry cocktail. You sip on it while I get the boat out of here."

"I don't think I can wait that long," she grinned as she accepted the martini glasses filled with the red liquid complete with dancing lime wedges on top.

"I doubt I can wait that long either," he whispered huskily. "But I'm thinking about the neighbors. They might call the police on us with all the noise that's going to be happening when I make love to you. I don't want us to be interrupted."

Jade swallowed at her excitement.

"Keep the cushions and yourself warm for me," he said and headed for the pilothouse.

Sipping on the cranberry cocktail, she savored the delicate combination of vodka, orange liqueur and sweet cranberries. When she was almost finished with her drink, she recognized the buzz of alcohol sifting through her brain and realized they were out of the marina, heading full speed for open waters.

No one was around but Caydon.

And he was watching her from the pilothouse with half-lidded lusty eyes.

Jade trembled.

Perhaps she should give the man a show.

She bit her lower lip thoughtfully. Did she have enough nerve to do what she wanted to do? Would she look like a fool dancing on the deck?

But why be shy?

She barely knew him. If she came off like an idiot, she'd probably never see him again anyway.

She grew painfully aware that she didn't want him to leave. She'd had such a lovely day shopping with him today, had exquisite sex with him last night and he'd even cooked for her.

Twice!

Maybe if she seduced him into staying at least for another day? Or maybe she could rig it so the engines wouldn't work and they couldn't return to shore, ever? Maybe she could make the keys disappear. Maybe she could make him fall in love with her.

Jade rolled her eyes and exhaled a frustrated breath.

He'd never fall in love with her.

He was just too sexy.

Too kind.

Too...poor?

That familiar niggle of doubt zipped through her. Was he trying to make her fall in love with him so he could go after her money like Beau had done? She wished she could stop thinking those suspicions.

Jade frowned as something else budged its way into her thoughts.

The other day when he'd first shown up to fix her engines, how had he started the boat while she'd slept? She always kept her key in her purse and the spare on a hook hidden deep inside one of the electrical consoles.

Had he gone through her purse? Maybe she'd left the key in the ignition? That would be the only explanation she could think of. She'd have to remember to ask him.

Later though.

Right now, the clamps were increasing in vibrations and really making her cream.

Looking over her shoulder, she found him smiling down at her and holding that little black box in the air.

The tease!

She would show him she could tease just as good as she got.

Taking a last swallow of the cranberry cocktail, she set it down on the deck nearby.

Remaining seated on the cushions, Jade made sure he was watching as she seductively slid her shirt over her shoulders and let it slip off her body.

* * * * *

The sexy way she slid her shirt off fired Caydon's blood. He didn't understand why he was so attracted to her. Didn't understand why every time he saw her he wanted to mount her, pleasure her, romance her.

Quite frankly at this point, he really didn't care.

All he wanted to do was go down to her, help her out of those clothes and bring her the pleasure she must be craving by now with those clamps he'd placed on her. But if he did that then he'd miss the show she was putting on.

And he didn't want to miss this.

He watched anxiously as she slipped her blouse off to reveal the sexy jade-colored teddiette he'd purchased for her. Her breasts looked firm and high beneath the lace. He could see the way her large nipples poked at the material compliments of the clamps he'd attached to her buds in the dressing room.

His mouth watered as he remembered taking her juicy nipples between his lips and plundering them. His cock hardened as he remembered reaching under the dining table in the restaurant to pinch and prepare her velvety labia for the clamps.

He'd loved the rapturous tremors that had sifted through her body as he'd intimately touched her soaked clit and brought her to orgasm right before dinner.

And now as she slid the teddiette straps over her bare arms, he clutched at the wheel of the yacht and inhaled sharply at the sight of her silky globes spilling free.

Reaching for a nearby switch, he turned on the floodlights illuminating her.

She lifted her arms up and hands tunneled through her shoulder-length hair.

His fingers suddenly ached to sift through her silky mass.

Beneath the bite-sized clamps, her flesh looked a dark rosy color nestled in large pink areolas. The silver chains and pink diamonds sparkled brilliantly under the floodlights.

She looked up at him and gave him a magnificent smile as if she were encouraging him to come on down and get her out of the rest of her clothes.

Caydon swallowed.

His cock shivered.

His body tensed.

He dragged in a shuddering breath.

Man, he hungered for her body in a dangerous way. So much so, that he almost forgot to shut the engines off in his haste to get out of the pilothouse and down to her.

When he reached her, she was standing on the deck.

Her body moved in a slow seductive dance.

Succulent breasts swayed.

Beneath her skirt, generous hips sensually gyrated.

By golly, he couldn't wait to rip the rest of her clothing off and plunge his thick cock into her.

* * * * *

The warm Florida air caressed her bared, clamped nipples as Jade danced in carefree circles on the deck. She could sense him behind her now. Could feel the heat of his powerful desire washing all around her. Her heart thudded against her chest. Need coiled like liquid fire inside her pussy.

When she finally stopped twirling, their eyes met.

Every nerve ending in her body shivered when she spotted his dark heavy-lidded gaze.

The man wanted to fuck her.

And she wanted to get fucked.

Good and hard.

Her head spun with excitement as he reached out to her.

Long masculine fingers curled around the elastic waistband of her skirt, branding her belly where he touched her naked skin.

"I've been waiting all day to touch you like this," he whispered as he knelt on his knees in front of her.

She swallowed as he began to roll her skirt over her hips, her knees. It fell to the deck in a silent hush. His hot tongue dipped into her belly button and she gasped at the sultry sensations shimmering through her lower abdomen.

At the same time, his hand slid between her legs and she felt the pinch of the clamps as he loosened them one at a time. Fire burned into her labia as the blood rushed back into the plump folds while he removed the clamps.

Oh God! She ached for him.

Her labia pulsed.

Her puffy clit quivered with a fierce need to be massaged and soothed.

His breath blew hot against her belly. His tongue teased her button, poking and swirling in the tiny cave until she inhaled ragged breaths.

"Caydon!" she found herself whispering. Her voice sounded tortured and desperate in her ears.

Reaching out she slid her hands to either side of his head, her fingers sifting through his feathery hair as she guided his face down between her legs. Her mind reeled as his tongue licked a burning streak of flames against her fine curly haired mons. Fever raged through her pussy as he drove a long finger deep inside her boiling channel.

Jade couldn't stop herself from arching her hips at the quick invasion.

Without warning he inserted another finger and yet another.

She inhaled a sharp breath as he slowly pulled the pleasure balls out of her. Then he reinserted his fingers, beginning a slow thrust, which threatened to destroy her.

Three fingers rammed into her, the sucking sounds shifted through the air.

Her soaked pussy dripped all around his plunging fingers. She was so wet for him, so eager to climax.

His head lifted and he looked at her. His face was flushed—his eyes a frantic bundle of need it just about made her have an orgasm on the spot.

"You're so tight, Jade. So unbelievably tight and so wet. I want to sink more of me into you," his voice sounded strangled. "I want to sink my whole fist into you."

The thought of having his fist buried inside her made Jade convulse in a frenzy of lust.

"Yes," she hissed. "Do me that way, Caydon. Do me. I need you inside me." She would do anything to have him in there.

Sweet sensations jumbled with pain as a fourth finger slipped inside. Her vaginal muscles ached with pleasure-pain.

She shivered at the large intrusion.

Her pussy burned.

Her mind fogged under the sexual torture.

His other hand slid between her legs. Masculine fingers pinched her aching labia, breathing more fire into her tormented flesh.

When he slid the calloused pad of his thumb over her sensitized pleasure nub, she climaxed.

Wailing under the harsh onslaught, she screamed out his name as the delicious storm of ecstasy took hold of her senses.

She bucked hard against his hand.

Moaned as his thumb seared against the spasming opening of her pussy.

Her pussy frantically clutched at this new intrusion as his thumb slipped inside.

My God!

His fingers and thumb filled her stretched her like she'd never been stretched before. Her entire body melted into acute sensual convulsions.

Her mind fragmented. Her legs went weak.

Jade's hands came off his head and landed on his broad shoulders, her arms felt like two trembling toothpicks ready to snap as she curled desperate fingers into his muscles in an effort to keep herself standing.

For a moment, she concentrated on the invasion. Concentrated on letting his entire fist inside.

But he didn't come in. His fist breeched her entrance.

"Too tight," he ground out. "This is as far as I can go."

Through heavy-lidded eyes, she watched the wondrous expression on his face as he stared between her legs. She could imagine him seeing his fingers and thumb disappearing into her. Could imagine how hot her juices must feel soaking his hand.

She sobbed hysterically as his knuckles rubbed and ground erotically against her sensitized clitoris.

Inside her pussy, a masculine finger massaged her G-spot.

Pleasure flowed through her whole body like a drug.

The sensations were unbelievable!

She threw her head back and let her hips gyrate on the massive penetration.

The orgasm made her cry. Made her laugh.

Made her scream out his name as she came all around his fingers and thumb.

The climax freed her like she'd never been freed before.

When it was over and he'd withdrawn from her, her legs gave out and Jade sagged against him like a limp rag doll.

He caught her in his strong arms.

With soothing whispers, he helped her onto the chaise mattresses she'd thrown earlier onto the deck.

Perspiration cooled her fevered flesh and his harsh breaths caressed her flushed cheeks.

She could smell her arousal as his wet masculine fingers sifted through her hair.

"Sleep, Jade. Sleep. When you wake up I have another surprise for you."

Did he say another surprise?

She wanted to ask him what he had in store for her next but when her eyes fluttered open, he wasn't there.

Jade sighed and snuggled into the mattresses.

Closing her eyes, she allowed her shuddering limbs to relax and listened to the gentle lapping of the ocean waves hitting the sides of her boat.

Did his surprise mean more sexual torture? Would he put more clamps on her nipples and labia? Or would he bring her more sex toys?

With a smile curving her lips, Jade fell into a slumberous sleep.

Chapter Seven

Christmas...

"Merry Christmas, sleepyhead."

A familiar masculine whisper into her ear made Jade's heart shoot into her throat.

She'd been fast asleep dreaming she'd been back on the slopes skiing at top speed, an ecstatic crowd encouraging her as she raced toward the finish line.

Crisp cold wind had slapped against her face, the sharp aroma of spruce gusting deep into her lungs. The scent of the forest had seemed so real. As if she were right there among the trees.

"Sleeping beauty, time for some more fun," he whispered again.

Opening her eyes she stared at the silhouette of a three-foot high spruce tree set in a huge white pot.

Pale blue miniature Christmas lights twinkled daintily along its branches.

Jade blinked and rubbed her eyes.

How odd, she thought sleepily, to have a fireplace and a Christmas tree beneath an open black sky filled with sparkling stars.

Under the blue glow of the lights on the tree, she noticed a scattering of presents.

She had to be dreaming.

"Wakey wakey, Jade. Time to decorate our tree."

Our tree?

"Caydon?" She turned her head to find him sitting on the deck beside her.

He wore a skimpy pair of bikini underwear laden with candy canes.

She couldn't stop her sharp inhalation at the quite impressive bulge pressing against the thin material.

His gorgeous smile slammed into her and she felt it as a wonderful punch to her gut.

In a flash, she remembered yesterday's events.

The pleasure balls. Shopping in the mall. Getting her nipples clamped in the dressing room, her labia clamped in the restaurant.

Coming back here to find the fireplace and then having wonderful sex.

And now a Christmas tree?

"Caydon? What are you doing?"

"Celebrating Christmas. It's midnight. Christmas is just starting. We have to get the tree decorated in her sexy garb."

Jade's mind whirled.

Decorate the tree? Celebrate Christmas?

Why would a man she barely knew want to celebrate Christmas with her? Why would he buy her Christmas presents and bring a real live Christmas tree onto her yacht?

She bit her tongue against the soaring questions just to make sure she wasn't dreaming.

Ouch!

She wasn't.

His grin widened. "Speechless?"

While she'd slept he'd turned off the spotlights, but in the shadows she noted his dark hair was damp and tangled. A fresh scent of soap wafted through the air as he leaned over her.

Obviously, he'd showered, probably a cold shower, thanks to her slumbering off on him.

Guilt zipped a solid line into her. It didn't take hold though as he intertwined his fingers with hers.

"Come on. Get up. Time to decorate our tree."

He pulled her to her feet with ease.

Helping her into the snug terrycloth robe he must have found in her bedroom, he led her over to a bunch of boxes piled on the nearby deck table.

"Ornaments. Lights. Even silver icicles. Do you know how hard it is to find silver icicles in Florida?" he laughed.

"How long did I sleep?"

"I come bearing you all kinds of gifts and all you are interested in is your beauty sleep?"

Jade cheeks grew hot. "That's not all I'm interested in," she replied truthfully.

"Decorate first. Fuck later."

He handed her a small open box.

Her heart pattered at the little copper glass balls that gleamed up at her. Adorned with tiny seed-sized pearls and sprayed with lines of spun sugar they were the prettiest things she'd ever seen.

"I'm so sorry I fell asleep on you," she found herself saying as the guilt returned.

He threw her a rather serious look. "You can sleep on top of me later. I let you sleep for a reason. I wanted you nice and rested for this momentous occasion."

"You take your Christmas decorating seriously don't you?"

"Very. And you are my captive until this tree is decked."

"Your captive? Hmm, I love the sound of that."

"After that I'll be yours. You can do with me what you want until your heart is guilt-free. Feel better?"

"Whatever I want?"

His eyes flashed with heat. "Anything you want."

He drew a string of amethyst beads out of a box, and started a slow whistle of a romantic Christmas tune and began to decorate the tree.

Just looking at his long masculine fingers as they draped the beads onto the spruce branches made Jade's pussy juices flow.

She'd made love to that gorgeous hand. Had gyrated her hips, pumped her slippery pussy all over it while he'd tried to fist-fuck her. The fist fucking hadn't worked but part of his hand had been inside her.

She exhaled roughly, as she remembered the fullness of him pushing into her.

His long thick fingers had explored her pussy, tenderly massaged her vagina and brought her to orgasm. Afterwards she'd simply collapsed and basked in her relief leaving him out in the cold.

Jade frowned.

His cock must be in one miserable hell as she continued to take pleasure from him and not give anything back.

It was time for her to give and for him to receive.

But first, they needed to decorate the tree.

* * * * *

Caydon didn't think he'd ever had so much fun decorating a tree. Or ever seen a prettier one even though it was only three feet tall.

Decked out in sprays of amethyst beads, gleaming copper balls, gold pinecones, miniature lights and silver icicles everything simply said Merry Christmas.

His whole life he'd enjoyed the Christmas season. Every year on Christmas Eve his grandfather Nonno, his pop and himself strolled into the hundred-acre woodlot his parents owned next to their grape farm in Tuscany, California and cut down a tree.

Laughter and cheers and play fights had abounded when they arrived home with their capture. After Nonno's careful trimming, everyone including his elderly grandmother participated in the decorating festivities at the stroke of midnight in order to hail in Christmas.

This year would be the first Christmas in his twenty-eight years that he wouldn't be celebrating with his family. Caydon smiled as he remembered telling his grandmother he might not be around this Christmas. He'd expected her to be disappointed, instead her watery blue eyes had sparkled happily, she'd clasped her hands together to her chest and cried out, "He's got a girl!"

Despite the fact he wouldn't make it home this Christmas, he wasn't the least bit sad. Gorgeous sexy Jade made up for his loss and she had turned out to be more than he'd ever dreamed. For the first time in his life, he felt totally at ease with a woman and had never felt so complete.

Hot feminine palms framed both sides of Caydon's naked waist and a beautiful velvety moist pressure slid along the back of his neck breaking him from his thoughts.

He grinned to himself.

His playful sex kitten was finally making her move. He'd seen the mischievous looks she'd thrown his way when she'd thought he was busily decorating the tree.

Every time he'd felt her hot gaze roving over his body, his cock had hardened and tightened just as it was doing now.

He turned around and caught site of her devilish grin a moment before she planted a pair of sexy soft lips right onto his mouth. She tasted so delicious, so warm and so tender that he quickly became lost in a flurry of his arousal.

His balls swelled and tightened until they were two solid glass ornaments ready to shatter.

When he tried to kiss her back, she pulled away leaving him with an odd sense of loss.

"You're up to something," he said as she reached for his wrist.

"Actually, you're the one who is up," she giggled.

He followed her gaze down to between his legs just in time to see her fingers from her other hand curl around his waistband and tug his candy cane underwear down over his hips.

His cock sprang free standing straight up against his belly as if were Santa Claus' North Pole ready to be mounted by a warm spasming pussy.

"You've been growing harder and harder as we decorated the tree and I've been getting wetter and wetter," she teased.

Her grin widened. "The tree is finished. Now it's your turn to be my captive."

"What an irresistible idea."

Caydon tried to reach out to grab her but something soft and tight snapped around his wrist. Before he could blink, he felt the same thing snap around his other wrist.

He looked down to find both his wrists handcuffed in front of him. "You're sneaky!"

She pouted prettily. "And so are you. Sneaking a Christmas tree on board with all these pretty looking presents."

"I can't help it if I like to surprise you."

"And I like to surprise you, too. I'll be right back." She disappeared from his view and the feeling of unease that had been haunting him on occasion since meeting her a couple of days ago quickly swept over him.

Cripes!

She looked so damned happy.

Happy and innocent.

Did she deserve him? A man who was far from innocent in the way of keeping why he was here a secret from her?

In fact, he was an asshole. A loser for not having guts and telling her the truth.

There was no absolutely no excuse not to tell her anymore. She would find out sooner or later from her sisters who he really was. When she did, it would be twice as bad as if he just spilled his guts now and took the fallout himself.

The handcuffs around his wrists suddenly made him feel more like a prisoner than a sexual captive. He yanked on them hard, suddenly wanting to be free, grimacing, as they stood strong.

"Why are you looking so worried?" she asked as she hobbled back onto the deck carrying a shopping bag.

Shit!

She'd ditched her terrycloth robe.

Totally naked she was bathed in pale moonlight, her beautiful
breasts bouncing joyfully with her uneven gait.

His cock hardened as he spied the light bush of curly hair hiding
her large labia and puffy clitoris from his view.

Her eyes sparkled with amusement. "Are you scared you might not
hold up under my sexual torture? You're mine now, Caydon Minnelli.
Totally mine. Want to see what I have for you here?"

He wanted to say no. Wanted to tell her to uncuff him so he could
break her heart.

Instead, he forced himself to smile as she urged him down onto the
mattresses dragging the big shopping bag with her.

"Hey, where'd you get that?" He nodded at the bag.

"When we split up in the mall you weren't the only one who was
planning surprises. I did my own Christmas shopping for you."

She'd shopped for him?

Soothing warmth washed away his shame at not telling her his
secret.

It was a good sign that she'd been thinking about him when they'd
been separated. Maybe this could all work out in the end?

"Are you ready to be sexually tortured?" she grinned.

"Throw me your best shot."

Slipping her hands into the bag, she busied herself unwrapping
whatever secrets the bag possessed.

When her hands came back out, his eyes widened with both shock
and arousal.

He couldn't stop the soft curse from escaping his mouth.

"It's a pussy sleeve. You like?"

"I don't know. Is it better than the real thing?"

She giggled. "How about I let you be the judge of that?"

Caydon swallowed at the sudden dryness in his mouth. He'd heard
the dangers of pussy sleeves. How they aroused a man to such heights

that there was nothing else around quite like it...except for the real thing.

What an absolutely delicious idea and it was making him harder by the minute.

"Look what else I have for you."

From her fingertips dangled something unmistakable.

Shit!

Payback was a bitch.

"Nipple clamps?"

"Just returning the favor. The saleslady said they work wonders on a man."

"I've never had nipple clamps before," he admitted truthfully.

Jade's green eyes blazed. "Neither did I, until the dressing room. Trust me you'll love them and you'll love this too."

Her perky breasts jiggled as she drew out a small bottle. Pouring some of the clear contents onto her palms, he recognized the mouth-watering scent of cinnamon caress his nostrils.

"What's that?"

"Sensual lube. Cinnamon Christmas Kiss is the scent. It'll heighten your senses."

"My senses are already heightened every time I look at you."

"Hmm. Compliments and flattery will get you everywhere but not out of what I have planned for you."

She rubbed her hands together, smearing the lube into her palms.

As she placed her hot little palms over his nipples, he couldn't stop the sudden erotic shuddering of his chest muscles. Her lube-soaked fingers spent a few minutes on each of his buds, sensuously sliding over them, tenderly stroking, pleasantly plumping and tweaking his flesh until they were firm, big beads of quivering flesh and he felt as if he might go mad from the shimmering sensations.

First, she clamped one drawn-out nipple and then the other, tightening the teeth until he inhaled sharply as they bit hard into his sensitized flesh. When she was finished, his engorged nipples burned as if they were on fire.

"You're right. It feels good to have my nipples clamped. Damn good," he groaned.

And it looked erotic as all hell watching a woman clamping him.

She threw him an "I told you so" smile and wrapped her hot little palms around the thick base of his cock where she began to massage more of the warm gel into his stiff flesh.

Oh boy!

His cock quivered beneath her burning touch. Automatically he arched his hips against her hands wanting more. His hunger for Jade increased.

"We've got to lube you up nicely," she whispered.

She looked at him from beneath long lashes, her mouth set in determination, her warm hands slurping this way and that way making his engorged flesh tingle erotically.

From tip to base, her sweet palms massaged his massive erection.

Silky feminine fingers roamed over the swollen mushroom-shaped head of his thick length making his entire body tighten magnificently with anticipation.

Fevered blood coursed up his shaft.

He groaned at the wild sensations.

His heart raced. His cock literally felt as if it were on fire.

"How's that feel?"

"Like I want to be fucked."

"Perfect. You're nice and wet. Just the way I want you."

"Touché." He grinned as he remembered using similar words on her.

She grabbed the red and white-stripped candy cane decorated pussy sleeve and leaned over him, her hair tumbling in front of her face, hiding her flushed cheeks from his view.

Apparently, she was enjoying this just as much as he was.

Her seductive scent swept around him, drugging him. Her breasts looked swollen as they swayed, her nipples hard with apparent arousal.

Positioning the opening of the pussy sleeve over the pulsing head of his engorged cock, she pulled it down over his slick swollen shaft.

The sleeve stretched around his thick head like a tight glove.

"Shit!" he hissed as powerful sensations made his abdominal muscles clench.

"It's got ribbing inside," she whispered.

Inside the pussy sleeve, he heard a slurping sound as she eased it down over his thick throbbing flesh.

He grimaced as rich bursts of pleasure shimmered all around him.

Interlacing the fingers of both hands around the pussy sleeve, she moved it up and down his slick cock.

The ribbed insides of the stretched pussy sleeve massaged and scratched the entire length of his swollen flesh sending sensual shards of lightning racing down his shaft and slamming into his balls.

Caydon groaned at the fantastic impact.

His arousal throbbed.

He felt the need to spew.

Clenching his jaws tightly, he held himself back and allowed the wonderful sensations to wash all around him.

His scrotum tightened.

His breath stalled in his lungs as she twisted mightily.

He cried out at the pleasure-pain.

Watched in awe as the swollen head of his cock peeked out at the top of the sleeve. A dribble of pre-cum beaded at the slit.

Jade leaned over.

With the tip of her pink tongue, she licked the beads off his throbbing head and moaned her approval.

The power of that sexy sound made his whole body tense. He wanted to plunge his raw burning cock deep into her supple warm pussy. Wanted to feel her soft body bucking beneath him as he drove into her tight slit over and over again.

The need to fuck was reflected in her eyes.

"Jade?" His voice sounded strangled, desperate.

She laughed as she enjoyed his sexual torture and he caught his breath at the tiny crinkles that erupted at the edges of her eyes.

Shit! He'd never noticed that before. Never noticed how beautiful she looked when she laughed.

And when her mouth opened and she could barely slide her lips around the pussy sleeve, he jolted as her hot tongue laved the entire head of his cock.

Sweet mercy, she was going to kill him!

Suddenly her hands were on his shoulders and she was pushing him onto his back.

He lay on the mattress, watching in awe as part of his cock disappeared into her mouth. Soft hands clenched around his scrotum, squeezing ever so gently, encouraging him to climax.

He couldn't stop himself from thrusting his hips upward into her mouth, an animalistic groan ripping from deep in his chest.

"Jade!" he gasped as the entire thick length of his rock-hard rod quivered its need.

Shoving his hips harder at her face, he felt her hot mouth tighten around the top of the pussy sleeve, the ribbing inside clenched ever so erotically around his rigid rod.

He tried to reach out to her but remembered his hands were cuffed.

"Mount me!" he cried out.

She slid the pussy sleeve off him.

His cock had grown so tight and so hard, he didn't know how long he could hold out.

She came over him like a goddess, her blonde hair flowing to her shoulders in wisps, the moon a halo around her head.

Her feet straddled both sides of his legs as she came down on him.

In the darkness he could imagine how her thighs were drenched with her arousal, could imagine how red and puffy her clitoris must look and how swollen her labia lips must feel.

Her eyes sparked heat as she straddled him.

He gritted his teeth as she teased his engorged cock-head with the tight opening of her hot pussy.

They both cried out as she dropped onto him, her wet pussy suctioning over his stiff flesh as if she were his very own hot pussy sleeve.

The current state of his impending release made him clench his eyes closed.

He cried out as he cut himself loose.

The explosion started in his balls, blades of white heat pounding into his shaft in a fierce blast that sent lights sparking behind his eyes.

He spewed his load right into her spasming pussy. He listened in awe to the suctioning sound of their juices mixing as her warm vagina sucked on his rigid cock eagerly draining him of his seed.

She rode him hard.

Her hips lifting.

Her hot pussy gripping him as she continued to slam down on his cock over and over again.

Her sexy moans mixed with his ragged groans as carnal sensations pierced his soul.

His mind swirled, his body spiraled beneath the waves of pleasure, leaving him dazed at the intensity.

When his orgasm died, he lay limp on the mattress, his harsh breaths tearing out of his lungs and shooting through the cool night air intermingling with her sensual whimpers of relief.

Tiny spasms from her vagina muscles continued to play with his softened cock as she kept him buried deep inside of her hot pussy and lay down on him, her soft feminine body curving over his rigid muscles.

Lifting his cuffed hands, he brought his arms around her head and down encircling her warm waist.

Her silky hair danced across his cheek and she nestled her head snugly into the curve between his shoulder and neck.

"I think I already love you." Her softly spoken whisper sliced through the air slamming into his ears, clutching warmly at his heart and leaving him so stunned he could only blink in wonder.

I think I already love you?

Had he heard right?

He waited for her to say it again but nothing came.

Should he say something? Should he tell her he knew he was in love with her? Should he tell her the truth about why he'd come here?

Seconds ticked away and he valiantly gathered his courage.

Yes, now was the time to tell her the truth. Now was the time to tell her he loved her.

"Jade?"

His answer was a soft snore.

Holy shit!

She'd fallen asleep on him.

In the afterglow of sex, people sometimes said things they meant or sometimes they said things they thought the other person wanted to hear.

But she had no idea that's what he wanted her to say to him.

She had no idea he'd fallen head over heels in love with her the instant he'd met with her two sisters and they'd told him things about her.

Like she was a kindhearted woman. Sensitive and loving.

Sexy as sin.

Well, the last part was his version.

Caydon smiled and cupped her curvy ass tightly with his handcuffed hands.

When she opened up her presents, he'd know if she loved him or not.

With that thought firmly in his mind, and Jade's juicy hot pussy wrapped tightly around his satisfied cock, Caydon drifted off to sleep.

* * * * *

Jade and Caydon made love again and again after they awoke at dawn.

They broke their lovemaking for breakfast and after that, they opened their Christmas presents.

Jade's heart had thumped wildly as his eyes lit up with both surprise and happiness as he eagerly ripped off the bows and shredded the cheerful Christmas wrappings she'd had professionally done while they'd been apart in the mall.

She'd gotten him a fishing rod, tackle box, a pair of cross-country skis, accompanying ski accessories and a generous gift certificate to a popular hardware store so he could purchase himself tools for his handyman trade.

In turn he'd given her things she'd need for a boat trip to Europe such as very detailed nautical maps of the ocean and Europe's waterways, an expensive compass-like object that he promised he would install on her yacht and some other nautical equipment her boat would need to get her to Europe.

There was a small fortune of equipment laying here on her deck. Stuff he couldn't afford on a handyman's salary. She wanted to tell him that he shouldn't have spent so much money on her. But she didn't want to offend him.

And he certainly wouldn't be getting her all these presents for her unless she meant something to him...or if he wanted to impress her...or he wanted something from her.

Uneasiness at the last unwanted idea made her frown.

Was Caydon another Beau? Did he want to buy his way into her graces in the hopes that he would have bigger fish to fry, so to speak, in the future?

Would she always look at every man as a potential Beau?

She had a couple of movie star friends who'd gotten taken in that way. Men who'd wined and dined them, made love to them, paid attention to them. Those attentive men had turned out to be gigolos or worse.

As the doubts rolled through her mind, Jade realized that her instincts were telling her to trust Caydon.

Caydon was not another Beau.

For years her instincts and Gram had told her not to trust Beau, she'd never listened.

Maybe it was about time she listened to herself.

"You're frowning. I don't think I like the looks of that."

"I thought you said it was too dangerous for me to go alone to Europe?"

"I did."

"So? What's with all this stuff?"

Her body tingled as he lifted her hands to his mouth and delicately kissed each sensitive fingertip one at a time.

"If you don't like these presents, I can take them back."

She caught the teasing glint in his eyes.

Trust him, Gram's voice echoed in her mind.

How could she trust a man she knew nothing about?

Sometime during last night when she'd made love to him she'd thought she might be in love with him. She might have even whispered it to him before she'd fallen asleep.

One thing she did know for sure though was she needed to trust a man sometime in her life and maybe the time to learn how to trust again was now.

"Well, I don't know if I want you to do that, Caydon. Maybe I'll need someone to show me how all this stuff works?"

Her pulse pounded and her body hummed as he stared at her.

She loved the intense way he looked at her. It was a look of caring, of joy, a look of confidence.

All those emotions couldn't be imitated.

Besides, her heart always burst with a warm fuzzy feeling at the sexy way his bangs blew over his forehead.

She really enjoyed the way he fucked her.

Dear God, had she truly fallen in love with him?

"Thought you'd never take the hint, Jade."

"What are you are saying? That you want to come along to Europe with me?"

"What I'm asking is do you want me to come with you? You said you wanted to go alone so I don't want to interfere in your quest for whatever it is you're looking for. If you'd rather go alone I'll stand by your decision and I'll make your yacht as safe as I possibly can. I am a handyman, y'know."

"You would leave your job and go off with me?"

This was the question she'd been dying to ask.

"I'm self-employed. I earn a very comfortable living. I can do whatever I want."

Jade relaxed. "I didn't know you were self-employed?"

A shiver of alarm zipped up her spine at the pained look that suddenly flooded into his eyes.

"Jade, there's a lot of things you don't know about me. Things I need to tell you..."

Desperation swooped over her and for some unknown reason she didn't want him to tell her anything right now. Things seemed just too good to be true. And she didn't want it to change.

"Caydon, I want you to make love to me. Right now."

That's exactly what he did.

Over and over again.

He kissed her so deeply—it took the breath clean out of her lungs. He entered her quivering pussy with a devastating slowness that made her cry out in arousal.

And he made love to her so exquisitely that he removed any lingering doubts she had about him.

Afterwards they returned to the Tampa Bay marina chatting gaily as they made plans to head off to Europe first thing New Year's Day.

Jade's newfound happiness however was short-lived.

It was that same afternoon when all those plans exploded...

Caydon's cell phone was ringing up a storm when Jade stepped out of the shower and spotted it lying on the bathroom counter. Obviously, he'd forgotten it when he'd showered earlier.

A family member was probably calling him to wish him a Merry Christmas.

She smiled as she listened to him whistling away with those Christmas tunes while he prepared a late lunch for them out in the kitchen.

The cell phone continued to ring with insistence.

"Caydon! Do you want me to get that?" she called out.

No answer.

He kept whistling.

The phone kept ringing.

Surely, he wouldn't mind if she answered it for him.

"Merry Christmas!" Jade chuckled into the phone.

"Hello? Who's this? Where's Caydon?" A woman's voice echoed in Jade's ears.

"Jade."

"Jade?" The woman sounded puzzled.

"Who's this?" Jade asked politely. Perhaps it was his sister? Or his mother?

Oh God! Not his mother! Not yet. How would she explain a strange woman answering her son's cell phone?

"Sandy, over at Kidnap Fantasies. Can you please get him for me? There seems to be an emergency here and..."

A cold wave blistered through Jade.

Kidnap Fantasies? What the hell?

From behind her, she barely heard Caydon's bare feet slap against the floor as he entered the bedroom.

"He's um...busy," she heard herself saying.

Kidnap Fantasies? Had she heard right?

Her ears began to ring. Her head started to spin.

"Would you please ask him to call me back when he's...finished with what he's doing."

Finished? Her stomach clenched.

Did she mean when he was finished fucking her? When he was finished his job?

Oh God!

Jade jumped when the bathroom door burst open and Caydon stepped into the steamy room.

He was naked.

His cock was engorged, and thick and quite ready to start fucking her again.

Nausea stung her stomach.

He reached out and playfully caught her by the arms pulling her backwards into his embrace. She barely felt his large hot hands cup her breasts. Ordinarily she'd be moaning against the erotic way his fingers tugged at her nipples but now she felt nothing but numbness.

"Hello? Jade?" The woman on the cell phone sounded impatient.

The cell phone trembled in her hand.

Kidnap Fantasies? Caydon worked for Kidnap Fantasies?

"Ma'am? Hello? Could you ask him to call me back? It's important."

"Um...sure."

"Fantastic. Merry Christmas!"

The line went dead.

Jade closed her eyes and tried to steady her frantic breathing. This couldn't be happening. It had to be some cruel joke.

Caydon worked for Kidnap Fantasies?

How could this be? She'd never mailed in that questionnaire.

"Who was it? A secret admirer I should be jealous of?" Caydon whispered against her ear.

"Kidnap Fantasies," she finally whispered.

Caydon's hands stilled on her breasts.

Even with the mirror fogged by steam of her shower, she could see his face pale.

"Oh God, I didn't want you to find out this way. I can explain."

If that reaction didn't confirm what that woman on the phone had said, then Jade was an idiot.

Ice slid into her veins.

"Don't bother explaining."

"Please, just listen to me."

"Get your hands off me!"

"Sweetheart, it isn't what you think."

Hot anger burst inside her like an explosion and Jade tore herself from his embrace.

"You bastard!"

He reached out to take her into his arms again but she slapped his hands away from her. The thought of him touching her sickened her. She wanted him gone. Wanted him out of her life!

Grabbing a towel, she quickly wrapped it around herself.

Humiliation made her hobble past him and she rushed out of the bathroom.

She needed air. She was going to pass out!

Blackness hovered at the edges of her sight and she stumbled through the bedroom.

She made it outside just in time. The warm afternoon breeze blew against her skin.

It helped, but only a little.

"Jade, I wanted to tell you."

Shit! He'd followed her out here? The prick had nerve!

She whirled around to face him. The need to strike him was so brutal she almost did it, but held herself back.

"You fuck women for a living?"

"No, it's not what you think."

The bastard was denying it. He was a liar. Just like Beau.

"Get off my fucking boat!"

"Sweetheart..."

"Get out of here, Caydon!"

"Please don't let it end this way," Caydon whispered.

No, this is not happening.

Her mind whirled. Caydon and Kidnap Fantasies?

He was still standing in front of her.

"Leave! I can't stand to see you. I don't want to ever see you again!"

His face whitened as if she'd struck him.

"Jade, I can't...I need to explain. I love you."

"Love? So soon? That's a joke! You're just like the rest of them. You're a loser. Just a gigolo."

"I can explain."

"Go away!" Hysteria edged into her mind. She felt like screaming. She'd do it too if he didn't leave.

She barely noticed a young couple on the nearby dock watching them.

He nodded. "Okay, take it easy. I'm going. Just take it easy. I'm going."

God! Why couldn't she cry? Why couldn't she slap him? Why couldn't she feel anything but this awful numbness? This horrible cold empty feeling?

She heard Caydon curse harshly as he jogged into the cabin.

A moment later, he erupted from the cabin wearing his jeans and pulling on his shirt.

"This doesn't change my feelings for you, Jade. I mean it when I say I love you."

"Go away. Please."

He didn't move. He stared at her long and hard.

She sensed he was expecting her to say something else but the numbness of shock was beginning to fade quickly being replaced by a pain so raw and ugly she didn't think she could survive it.

Regret, confusion and a dozen other emotions she couldn't put a name to flashed in his blue eyes.

"I love you, Jade Hart," he whispered.

Through suddenly welling tears, Jade watched as he turned and left.

Her legs trembled violently. Her stomach continued to clench with waves of nausea.

She closed her eyes and grabbed the steel railing for support.

What in the world was she going to do now?

His cell phone began to ring again.

Her eyes snapped open.

She couldn't bear to answer it. With shaky fingers, she dropped it over the edge of the yacht.

It hit the water with a splash.

The twinkling lights on their little Christmas tree caught her attention.

Fury, rich and violent slammed through her. Without thinking, she grabbed at a prickly branch. She barely felt the tingling pain of the spruce needles biting into her flesh.

Lifting the tree, she hoisted it overboard.

When she heard the giant splash, it seemed as if a dam suddenly tore lose inside her.

Anger, pain and other gut-wrenching emotions spun through her like a whirlwind. Jade slumped onto the deck amongst the strewn Christmas wrappings and presents they'd opened.

Frantically she wiped at the tears of hurt spilling down her face. Tears of pain that were breaking her heart. Suddenly she realized she was once again alone at Christmas. Just like she'd been last year when Beau had left her.

Chapter Eight

New Years Eve morning...

Jade had just paid and sent away the man who'd delivered all the boxes of dried goods and other things she'd need for her yacht trip to Europe when she heard the phone ring.

She debated whether she should answer it or not. Caydon had called many times over the past few days. Every time she'd seen his name appear on the caller ID screen of her phone she'd burst into another round of tears.

A quick glance at the ID screen showed it wasn't Caydon calling this time but her sister Jillian along with Johnna.

They were bearing down on her with a conference call.

Her anger burned even brighter.

Over the past few days, she'd figured it all out. Jillian and Johnna's unexpected visit. Both of them getting her curiosity aroused so she'd fill out the Kidnap Fantasies questionnaire. Then the questionnaire had disappeared shortly afterwards.

They'd somehow taken it and sent it to the organization.

And the organization had sent Caydon Minnelli, biggest cock in stock.

But why would Caydon buy her all that expensive nautical equipment for Christmas? Why invite himself to come along on her trip?

The only thing that made sense was her theory about him wanting to ingratiate his way into her life so he could get some sort of relationship going and get her money. Somehow, before he'd even met her he'd found out about her dream trip and used it to his advantage.

She should have figured that out easily enough simply by realizing he bought all those presents even before she'd told him about her dream of sailing to Europe.

Her sisters must have been the ones to tell him where she'd kept the keys to start her boat so he could "kidnap" her. But why would they tell him about her dream trip?

"You must have had a really good laugh reading my private fantasies." Jade hissed into her cell phone after flicking it on.

"Jade! I'm so sorry. We never read it." Jillian sounded very upset. Served her right.

"It's all my fault what happened between you and Caydon," she continued. "If I'd just told you right up front and not taken that questionnaire to him everything would have worked out fine."

Jade's senses whirled.

"You met him?"

"We both met him," Johnna chimed in. "We had to check out the merchandise to make sure he was suitable for you."

Oh my God! What was she hearing? Her two sisters had actually gone to meet the guy who would ultimately fuck her?

Insanity!

"Sis? You still there?" Jillian asked softly.

"She's still there," Johnna chuckled. "She can't stay mad at Caydon or us for long. Not after everything we had to go through to get them together. And boy you're going to want to hear what Jillian had to do..."

"I don't want to know."

"Caydon Minnelli came to me in a dream I had one night not too long ago," Jillian said softly.

A shiver of uneasiness zipped through Jade. Over the past two years, Jillian had sworn she'd had premonition like dreams. She'd even seen how Johnna and Jeff had found each other weeks before they'd met.

"You saw him in one of your dreams?" Jade asked, awed for a moment.

"That's why we sent him to you, because it's fate," Johnna said.

"Well, not this time," Jade snapped, as the familiar anger churned inside her chest. "As far as I'm concerned Caydon Minnelli can go straight to hell."

"Would it help if I told you that I tried very hard to persuade him to meet you?" Jillian said. "He told me he didn't believe in my dreams and that although he'd been infatuated with you while watching you on television, he didn't want to meet you."

"He lied. He met me."

"He was intrigued by your questionnaire."

"Forget the questionnaire! He's a boy toy. I can't be with a man who fucks women for a living!"

"Jade!" Johnna's stern voice hauled in her mounting anxiety. "That's uncalled for. Jillian was following through on her dream."

"Well, I'm sorry but I didn't ask for her help. And I didn't ask to fall in love with another gigolo."

"You're in love?" Johnna said gently.

"A gigolo?" Jillian asked.

Tears of frustration welled up and Jade couldn't stop the frustrated sob from breaking free of her chest.

"Oh great, now we made her cry." Johnna sounded upset.

"Why do you think he's a gigolo? He's absolutely nothing like Beau." Jillian said.

"For crying out loud! He works for Kidnap Fantasies. He makes love to other women for a living."

"Works for KF? He doesn't work for them." Johnna blurted out.

"He owns it. Actually he is a part-owner," Jillian said.

"Owns it?" Jade hiccupped.

"He's a self-made millionaire," Jillian explained. "He owns a string of hardware stores across the States and he invested in KF. Do you know how hard it was for me to even track him down and to get him to trust me enough to explain about my dream about him and you meeting through Kidnap Fantasies?"

Curiosity was beginning to edge away Jade's anxiety. Caydon didn't work for that...company. He was a part-owner?

"When I saw the name Kidnap Fantasies in my dream, I remembered seeing it written down somewhere. I went through Gram's old stuff we kept and found a paper with a letterhead that belonged to Gram's lawyer. On that paper was someone's scrawled handwriting, which said Kidnap Fantasies. I don't know who wrote it down or why, but I took the paper to the lawyer, told him about my dream and that I needed to find Kidnap Fantasies."

"And he told you he could help you?"

"No, he told me I was totally crazy. He told me to get lost before he called security."

"What did you do?" Jade asked.

"I informed him I wouldn't leave until he produced information about this Kidnap Fantasies. So I...handcuffed myself to his desk."

"You didn't!"

"She did!" Johnna laughed.

"And you know what happened after that?" Jillian asked.

"He told you Caydon's name."

"No. He left the office to go and get the security guard. I wasn't there one minute when the man in my dream walked into the office. Caydon's face went so pale at seeing me handcuffed I thought he might pass out from shock," Jillian giggled.

Jade could barely suppress her laughter at what Caydon must have thought seeing her sister cuffed to his grandfather's desk.

"What did he do?"

"He wasn't amused," Jillian explained. "He thought his grandfather and I were doing something kinky behind his grandmother's back. Then I explained everything about my dream and showed him the paper with the scrawled handwriting that said Kidnap Fantasies on it and then I showed him your picture, remember the one on the cover of

People magazine? That's when he told me what I was telling him was so unbelievable it just might be true. And you know what else?"

"What?"

"He couldn't take his eyes off your picture. His eyes just lit up when he looked at you. It was like he recognized you. Even when he was saying there was no way he was going to meet you based on my story he kept staring at your picture. In the end, he set up a meeting between the two of us where he handed me that brochure of Kidnap Fantasies and a questionnaire for you. The rest is history."

"You told him about my dream trip to Europe?"

"Guilty," Jillian replied. "I had to tell him what a wonderful person you are and that included your dreams."

"So? Are you going to make up with him?" Hope filled Johnna's voice.

"I...I don't know where he is," Jade admitted.

Her Caller ID didn't display a person's number just their name.

Not to mention the way she'd kicked him off her boat on Christmas Day telling him she never wanted to see him again, he might not want to see her again.

"I have his phone numbers," Jillian sang.

"Oh Jade, go for it," Johnna urged. "You've already admitted you're in love with him."

Jade swallowed at her blooming excitement. "Okay, give me the numbers."

After getting his numbers and the promise she'd call Caydon, Jade broke the conference call with her sisters.

Slumping into a nearby deck chair, she gazed at the electric fireplace that had been too heavy to chuck overboard with the Christmas tree.

Caydon was an owner of Kidnap Fantasies? What kind of a man would be part of that type of a business? And why?

She frowned when she spotted something glinting off a string from one of the still filled Christmas stockings that hung off the mantle of the fireplace.

"What in the world?" Jade whispered as she stood.

Drawing closer to it, her mouth went dry with shock and she thought she just might start bawling right then and there.

Fluttering in the warm Florida breeze and tied to a pretty piece of gold tinsel was a big fat pink diamond ring.

Chapter Nine

Fifteen minutes before New Year's...

"Come on, Caydon, answer your damned phone," Jade grumbled anxiously into her cell phone as she lay in bed holding her hand up to the window admiring how the full moon's rays sparkled against the pink diamond ring she'd slipped on her finger.

She'd been calling Caydon off and on since Jillian had given her the numbers. Earlier this morning she'd actually had him on the line but at the sound of his sexy voice she'd chickened out and hung up on him.

When she'd gathered up the nerve to try again she hadn't been able to get an answer anywhere. Not at his office, his pager or his home.

She'd wanted to apologize to him for her being such a bitch and not letting him explain. But she'd been hurt and humiliated by the telephone conversation with that Kidnap Fantasies woman.

Most of all she didn't like the fact he'd lied to her.

It had felt like Beau all over again. Lying to her. Hanging around her simply so he could manage her money and her career.

But Jillian had said Caydon had his own money. So, he wasn't interested in hers. But what if he'd been dirt-poor? Would that have made her want to apologize to him? Want him back in her life?

Jade sighed.

She didn't know the answer to that question.

Poor or rich, all she knew was that over the last few days she'd missed her sexy man terribly and now she couldn't even find him.

As she watched the ring glisten in the moonlight, a fluttery happy feeling clenched the pit of her belly.

The pink diamond on this ring looked like the same type as the tiny diamonds that dangled off those nipple clamps and labia clamps he'd outfitted her with.

Had he been planning a proposal all along?

It sounded so insane and yet maybe, just maybe, Caydon Minnelli was interested in her. After all, he was interested enough in the questionnaire to come and meet her in the first place.

What about the ring though?

He wouldn't have tied this pretty ring to a piece of tinsel and hung it from her stocking if he wasn't serious about her. Right?

Jade frowned.

She'd ruined everything by not letting him explain. Ruined his plans to propose.

Swearing softly into the silence she flipped the cell phone closed and set it on the bed beside her.

It could be that he wasn't answering on purpose.

Maybe he'd changed his mind and didn't want anything more to do with her? Maybe she was being silly thinking that he wanted her after the way she'd freaked out and sent him packing.

Or she was just being dumb by keeping this pretty rock on her finger when she'd have to send it back to him anyway.

Oh, but it was so pretty.

She shouldn't keep it, though. It wasn't right.

She tried to slide the ring off her finger but it didn't budge.

Great! Just what she needed.

She pulled harder.

Nothing.

She twisted it this way and that. Still nothing.

By golly, it felt as if it had been cemented onto her finger.

A slice of laughter slipped past her lips at the thought of having to have her finger cut off just so she could send him back the ring.

Suddenly she spotted a flash through the window high in the sky.

"A falling star!"

Quick! Make a wish! Gram's voice sailed softly through her mind.

"I want Caydon, Gram," Jade whispered longingly into the quiet of New Year's Eve. "I want Caydon back in my life."

The star disintegrated.

At that same instant, she heard the rumble of engines come to life. For a second she thought the owners to the yacht docked next to hers were heading out to celebrate New Year's. But she didn't see any lights on.

Then her yacht swayed just a little.

A gut-wrenching feeling clutched her gut as she felt her boat begin to move.

Oh my goodness someone was stealing her boat!

With her in it!

Fumbling in the moon glow, she struggled to find the cell phone. The instant her hand touched the cool item she heard the soft sound of familiar whistling.

It was a New Year's tune.

It took Jade only moments to locate her robe and cane and hobble down the hallway, through the kitchen and out onto the main deck into the salt-scented ocean air. Maneuvering quickly and quietly up the stairs, she then entered the dimly lit glass-enclosed pilothouse.

Caydon Minnelli stood at the computer console. His legs slightly spread. His long fingers curled around the captain's wheel. His broad back was to her as he looked out the window and carefully steered the yacht out of the berth.

And he was totally naked!

His musky masculine scent drifted to her along the fresh ocean breeze teasing her nostrils. She couldn't stop the delicious lashes of lust from uncurling deep in her pussy as she savored the sight of his nice plump ass cheeks ready to be cupped into her eager hands.

However, she didn't dare touch him or press herself against his magnificent nude body.

At least not yet.

"I'd recognize that cute ass, anywhere," she whispered.

He stiffened in surprise, obviously unaware she'd come into the pilothouse. He stopped whistling and turned his face toward her.

His appearance shocked her.

Dark stubble stained his face, dark shadows haunted his eyes and there was an uncertainty in the way he held himself.

If she didn't know any better she'd swear the man had missed her. Maybe even pined over her?

She swallowed at the bright lust shining in his eyes and the sight of his nostrils flaring as he smelled the air.

"And I'd recognize the sweet scent of your arousal anywhere."

A shiver of anticipation raced up her back.

"You've got balls coming back here, Caydon Minnelli."

"Rock-hard balls, baby. Real solid and ready to spill deep into your sweet pussy."

Jade's pussy dripped with cream at his words.

She wanted him to fuck her. Wanted to feel his swollen shaft slide deep into her aching pussy. Wanted it more than her next breath.

"So?" he continued as he turned back around and maneuvered her yacht between the gently bobbing buoys that guided them out of the marina. "How come you've been calling me all day?"

Son of a bitch!

"Why didn't you answer?"

"And give you the chance to hang up again? No way."

"Why would I call and then hang up?"

"Because you did it once this morning when I answered. I wasn't going to let you get cold feet again."

"I didn't get cold feet."

"So what would you call it?"

"Changing my mind."

"I hear it's a woman's prerogative." There was a teasing chuckle in his voice. "So why'd you call me?"

"To apologize."

"I flew all the way out here for a simple apology?"

"That's all I'm prepared to give you at this point in time, Caydon."

Liar! Gram's voice whispered in her ear as plain as if she were in the pilothouse with them.

"So, I guess you've wasted a trip."

"Actually, Jade, I came all this way to kidnap you. And that's what I intend to do."

Jade's pulse picked up speed.

"And I came all this way to tell you that I should I have told you the truth right from the start."

"Why didn't you?"

He shook his head slowly. "I don't know. After your sisters gave me your questionnaire, I realized I really wanted to meet you. But I wanted it to happen naturally between us, not because we were forced to meet. Jillian explained her dream and I thought maybe you'd think we belonged together because of her premonition. I wanted to tell you why I had come. I tried...but I just couldn't. I had to believe it was natural between us."

"God! What we have together is very natural." Jade laughed as she walked up behind him and slid her arms around his lean waist. Muscles bulged against her fingers as she trailed downward and dove beneath his long hard cock to cup his swollen balls nestled in his tight sac.

He sucked in an aroused breath.

"What we have together can't be faked, Caydon. The minute I saw you standing there watching me, something inside my heart shifted into place. At the time, I wouldn't admit it. I couldn't admit that a guy might be interested in me...at least not the way I am with my leg and hip..."

"I think we covered all that, Jade." He pressed his warm ass backward against her belly.

Her cheeks grew warm at the thought that Caydon wanted her just the way she was.

"I know, I know. You suffer from the lady in distress syndrome."

"And by the way you're grabbing at my balls and the way your nipples are poking into my back, I'd say you're getting pretty distressed, Jade."

He grabbed her hands, pulled her fingers from his rock-hard balls and swung her in front of him, holding her against him as he now stood behind her. This time it was her turn to nestle her ass against him. His rock-hard cock pressed against the thin material barely clothing the crack in her ass cheeks.

"I do believe I have a remedy for your distress," he whispered.

His fingers intertwined with hers and he placed her hands on the steering wheel of her boat. "And you put it on your finger without giving me a chance to pop the question."

My goodness! She'd forgotten to take it off.

"I was just trying it on...and it got stuck."

"Stuck, huh?"

"Well, you try to take it off and see what I mean."

"Maybe it won't come off for a reason," he chuckled. "Maybe it's that falling star I saw a minute earlier. Maybe my wish of us being together is going to come true."

"That's the same wish I made when I saw it tonight," Jade whispered in awe.

"They always say if two people wish on the same star and for the same thing it'll come true for sure," Caydon said.

"No wish is going to come true until you tell me one thing."

He kissed the curve of her neck unleashing delicious little tingles through her body.

"What do you want to know?"

"This Kidnap Fantasies, what exactly is it?"

"Top secret."

"So I've heard."

Her eyes widened as she felt something clamp around one wrist and then the other.

Shit! He'd handcuffed her to the steering wheel!

"You steer. I have other business to attend to."

Pure desire ripped through her veins as his fingers untied the sash on her robe. Warm air brushed her curves as he lifted the material over her hips and tied it into place with the sash so it wouldn't fall down.

"Tell me about it, Caydon. I want to know why you'd invent something like that?"

His hands settled on the curves of her hips. His hot breath embraced her ass.

"First of all, Sandy, the woman who you spoke with on my cell phone is relatively new at Kidnap Fantasies. She was given my private number over the holidays in case she couldn't reach the other partners. She shouldn't have revealed the organization to you without verifying if you were a client. Only a select few know about it. She's been...reprimanded."

"Reprimanded? How?"

His hands smoothed tenderly over her ass cheeks. "Let's just say she's paid very well to follow orders...she won't forget this lesson. As to Kidnap Fantasies, I only invested in it. My partners invented it and they run it. They have personal reasons why they're doing what they're doing."

"So you really don't participate with..."

"With other women?" He gently bit into her ass cheek making Jade squirm from the sting of pain.

"Everything I told you was the truth. I'm not married and I've never wanted to be with a woman so badly as I want to be with you. When I saw your picture on the cover of that magazine that your sister showed me I was shocked that I might have an opportunity to actually meet you. When I read your Kidnap Fantasies questionnaire about you wanting a big cock and that you were open to new sexual experiences

I just knew I had to meet you and make some of your fantasies come true."

"Now that you've kidnapped me and handcuffed me to my boat's steering wheel, where are you taking me? A secret island where you can fuck me 24/7?"

"If you call your yacht an island on the ocean."

"What are you saying, Caydon?"

Dare she hope? Dare she hope that he would say he wanted to come with her?

She held her breath as she awaited his answer

"I'm saying I'll be fucking you 24/7 all the way to Europe...if you want me to come?"

Her heart tripped wonderfully. "I want you to come all right. Inside me. Now."

"I can arrange that."

She couldn't stop the whimper of her excitement as she caught the reflection in the pilothouse window of him standing up behind her.

His hand slipped beneath her handcuffed arm and came around to settle over the swell of her belly. He pulled her back a couple of steps then instructed her to bend over.

She cried out as his hot fingers slipped between her legs and he pried her fat labia lips apart, his finger finding her swollen clitoris. With a firm pressure, he began a leisurely massage.

"Oh Caydon, yes. That feels so good," she whimpered.

"Just good?"

A finger slipped inside her vagina making her gasp her answer.

Heat scorched her skin. Her nerve endings flared to life. Her head spun.

The finger on her pleasure nub increased in pressure sending Jade's body spiraling toward her pleasure.

He continued to knead her clit and she strained her hips backward pushing herself harder against his hand.

"There, that's the way I want you. Nice and wet and ready for me."

Delicious shivers rampaged through her body as his stiff swollen cock probed against the opening of her drenched pussy.

"Ready and willing to be fucked whenever I want it."

"How about when I want it?" she breathed.

"That won't be a problem. You want it all the time," he chuckled hoarsely. "Just like I want you all the time. Now brace yourself."

Before she had a chance to heed his warning and tighten her grip on the helm, he speared his long thick cock into her with one solid thrust burying himself right to the hilt, his hard balls slamming into her ass.

She cried out at the shocking impact. Her legs buckled and she fought to steady herself as he impaled her on his cock.

He stretched her open so wide her eyes teared up.

"Better than good?" he whispered in a tortured voice.

"Much," she gasped as her pussy walls clenched tightly around the long thick invasion.

"So what did you wish for that first night we saw our falling star?" he said between gritted teeth as he slid out and then sliced his solid erection into her slit burying himself right to the hilt again.

She wasn't the least bit embarrassed to tell him, especially now that his delicious cock was doing such wondrous things to her.

"A trip to Europe...with you as my personal love slave on my yacht," she confessed.

"Your love slave? Really?"

"You sound surprised," Jade breathed against the pleasure threatening to swallow her whole.

"I had a similar wish." Caydon groaned as her vagina began to quiver around his intrusion. "I wished you would turn out to be the one."

Happiness washed over her. Through blurry tears, she looked at the pink diamond sparkling on her finger.

"I think I am the one...if Jillian's vision and this ring is any indication. I can't seem to get it off my finger. So you won't be getting it back unless you want my finger too."

"I want your finger and all of you. Will you marry me when we get to Europe? Will you be my wife? Will you have my babies?"

"If you keep fucking me this hard we'll have one before we even get there," Jade laughed. She couldn't believe she'd just said that. Having babies with a guy she barely knew was just nuts. But it felt so right saying it and doing it.

In the window, she saw his eyes flash with lust. His teeth clenched as he slammed his hips and penetrated her even deeper.

Jade hissed at the pleasure-pain as his cock slammed into her again.

"You didn't answer my question. Will you marry me?"

She resisted the urge to close her eyes and sink into the pleasure. She wanted just one more moment with his reflection.

"Yes, I'll marry you."

A wonderful grin curled the edges of his lips.

"Happy New Year, Jade."

"Happy New Year, Caydon," she whispered back as her pussy clenched tighter around his enormous shaft and his finger continued to massage her clit.

Her last thought before she spiraled into her orgasm was she was really going to enjoy making babies with Caydon Minnelli.

She was going to enjoy it.

A lot.

The End

Newsletter

Hi! If you would like to get an email when my books are released, you can sign up here:

Newsletter: http://ymlp.com/xguembmugmgb

Your emails will never be shared and you can unsubscribe whenever you like.

For more ebooks and print books please visit http://www.janspringer.com

Want more Jan Springer Adult Romances?

Mini Catalog

Book Two
Christmas Lovers
(can also be found in the Merry Ménage Kisses Boxed Set)
Sergeant Connor Jordan, wounded overseas and sent back to the States to recuperate, just cannot stop fantasizing about the sexy nurse who cared for him. When his brothers give him a holiday gift certificate to Kidnap Fantasies, a top-secret fantasy organization, Connor knows he'll use their gift, if only to help him forget his wickedly delicious attraction to Nurse Sparks.
Nurse Tania Sparks has always been purely professional with her injured soldiers...until sinfully sexy Connor Jordan enters her hospital. He makes her body throb with an intense desire she's never known before. The last thing she wants is to get involved with the injured warrior. So what's a woman supposed to do to relieve her naughty frustrations? Call Kidnap Fantasies and have them supply her with a look-alike man who'll help her forget her sexy soldier...

When Tania and Connor unexpectedly come together at a secluded mountain chalet, their love explodes in a ménage of passion, sensuous desires and a happily forever after.

Contains ménage scenes.

Book Three

Zero to Sexy

Because Santana hides from something bad in his past he lives only for the moment and doesn't dare dream of a future. He exists within the sensual world of Kidnap Fantasies, a top-secret escort world where he explores his sexuality and enjoys pleasure with both men and women. But it is love at first sight the instant he sees Amy at his good friend's wedding. She's got future written all over her. He knows she is a hunger he must deny, so why is he whispering "you're mine" to her at the wedding?

The instant Amy Sparks sees the handsome African American at her sister's wedding, she knows in her heart that he's everything she's ever fantasized about in a lover, but before they can connect, he mysteriously disappears. Upon discovering he works for Kidnap Fantasies, she knows how he'll make all her intimate fantasies come true...

When Santana's next Kidnap Fantasies assignment turns out to be Amy, he knows he must protect her from his past and he can be with her only this one time...

Reader Advisory: Includes a sizzling ménage scene and some male on male sensual interaction.

Boxed Sets

SIX Erotic Romance Ménage Stories! INCLUDES A BONUS MÉNAGE EBOOK

BONUS Ménage BOOK "Cowboys for Christmas" book 1 of Jan's new Cowboys Online series. Jennifer Jane is getting THREE Cowboys for Christmas ~ What more could a girl want? Jennifer Jane Watson has spent the past ten Christmases in a maximum-security prison. The last thing she expects is to get early parole along with a job on a secluded Canadian cattle ranch serving Christmas holiday dinners to three of the sexiest cowboys she's ever met!

~

Step into The Key Club's Ménage Nights where naughty fantasies come true and two men are hotter than one. Includes FIVE bestselling The Key Club stories; Ménage, Marley's Ménage, A Merry Ménage Christmas, Sophie's Ménage and Jewel's Ménage.

The Key Club Series
Ménage - Book One

Sandwiched between constant deadlines, erotic romance author, Claire Miller, enjoys an occasional unwind at The Key Club...this time she's going to indulge in a yummy ménage.

Marley's Ménage - Book Two

Single soon-to-be mom Marley Madison has had some wicked cravings in her day, but being pregnant has made her cravings downright...naughty. She wants a sizzling ménage and she needs it bad.

A Merry Ménage Christmas - Book Three

Dr. Kelsie Madison can't remember the last time she's had no-strings sex and that's her clue she's been working way too hard. It's time to unwind at the Key Club by indulging in a yummy Christmas present for herself...a red-hot ménage.

Sophie's Ménage - Book Four

It's Spank-Me Ménage Night at the Key Club and Sophie is finally taking the plunge back into the spank scene...she didn't expect her two ex-boyfriends to be there too.

Jewel's Ménage - Book Five

She thought she would never trust a man again...
Until one rainy night two hunky truckers come to Jewel's rescue,
igniting delicious desires for a red-hot ménage a trios.
Jaxie's Ménage - Book Six

A close encounter with death pushes Jaxie into making one of her
most intimate fantasies come true...
A Homecoming Ménage Christmas - Book Seven

Rachel has a very naughty secret and she's way too embarrassed to let anyone know about it. When The Key Club throws a Santa Fetish Ménage Night, it's almost too good to be true. She has to figure out how to participate without anyone finding out!

Pleasure Bound Box Set
The Complete Series
Books 1 - 6

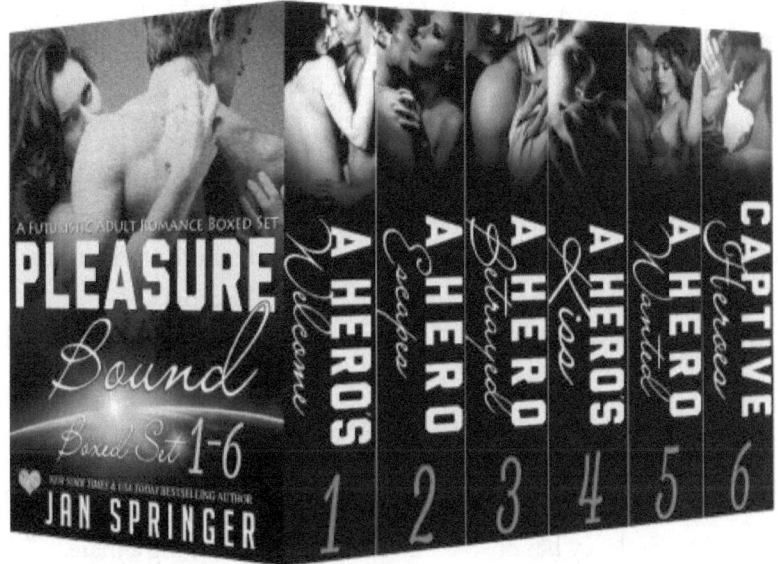

A Futuristic Adult Romance
Books 1-6

This PLEASURE BOUND BOXED SET is an EROTIC ROMANCE and includes the first SIX books in the Pleasure Bound series.

TOP-SECRET MISSION: Explore a recently discovered planet in outer space.

DISCOVERY: A sizzling trip into the realms of bondage, bdsm, pleasure-pain, betrayal and...love.

Inside this Boxed Set:

During a top-secret mission to a newly discovered planet, the six Hero siblings are thrust into a sensual world of erotic violence, unconventional romance and sizzling sex.

A HERO'S WELCOME
Pleasure Bound Book One

Jan Springer

Being shot and held captive isn't what astronaut Joe Hero had in mind when he agreed to a top-secret mission to explore a newly discovered planet for NASA.

But a man would have to be dead not to fall for the sensual female doctor in charge of his care.

One night of scorching passion in the arms of the stranger from another planet is enough to convince Dr. Annie there's more to males than she's been taught by the Educators.

Who is this sexy hunk and why does she welcome him into her bed and her heart *every* chance she gets?

A HERO ESCAPES
Pleasure Bound Book Two

Jan Springer

Queen Jacey has always fantasized about bedding a male.

But taking one for her enjoyment is strictly forbidden. That is, until an attractive well-hung stranger from another planet forces her to overcome her training and her beliefs.

Being held captive and forced to mate with a gorgeous Queen isn't exactly what astronaut Ben Hero expected when he agreed to explore a newly discovered planet for NASA.

Escaping *should* be his top priority but making sizzling love to Jacey *is* all he can think about.

When he discovers she's also being held captive, Ben's protective instincts kick in big time.

Suddenly they're on the run, irresistibly aroused, and wrapped in each other's arms every chance they get!

A HERO BETRAYED
Pleasure Bound Book Three
Jan Springer

Astronaut Buck Hero didn't count on being held captive or becoming infected with passion poison when he agreed to explore a newly discovered planet for NASA.

If he doesn't get the cure soon he's going to be one *very* dead man. Fugitive on-the-run Virgin has just rescued an infected male and needs to administer the cure - a twenty-four-hour sex marathon. Then she'll turn him over to his enemies in order to gain her freedom.

But her well-laid plans go into orbit when she discovers she's fallen in love with the stranger from another world.

A HERO'S KISS
Pleasure Bound Book Four
Jan Springer

During a secret NASA mission to locate their brothers on the faraway planet of Paradise, the Hero sisters become separated after they crash land...and find unexpected romance with the tormented male warriors of the species.

Jarod and Piper

Being injured and infected by sensuous swamp water isn't what Piper Hero signed up for when she agreed to search for her three missing brothers. But when she's rescued by a dangerously sexy man who makes her so hot that she can't even think straight, Piper is glad that she came.

Jarod Ellis has sworn off women. But he's captivated by Piper Hero, a woman who claims to be related to the Earthmen he has vowed to protect with his life. Although he mistrusts her, she sets free a carnal inferno of needs he's never experienced during his previous life as a pleasure slave.

Despite her intimate fantasies coming true, Piper knows she needs to continue her mission of reuniting her siblings and she'll do it-with or without the help of her well-hung stud...

A HERO WANTED
Pleasure Bound Book Five
(Loosely connected with this series)
Jan Springer

Old-fashioned gal needs a man who loves to walk in the rain. Must be well-hung. A homebody, white picket fence-type of guy. Sexual requirements-gentle yet untamed lover. He must be sexually adventurous who will train me to be same. Must be romantic, enjoy toys, interested in mutual light bondage, ménages are welcome.

That's what full-figured, antiques shop owner Jenna MacLean wants when she and her best friend outline a want ad just for fun on their weekly girls' night out.

After years of being away from his pretty-plus sized ex-girlfriend, Sully's back in town. When he finds the want ad, he knows he's the only man who can make all of Jenna's sizzling-hot fantasies come true. She's never left his heart and he needs her back in his bed-but he's not going the traditional romantic route. This time, he'll prove he loves her with help from the notorious Ménage Club, a relationship club designed specifically to get estranged couples back together with the help of a third and sometimes a fourth in the bedroom.

CAPTIVE HEROES
Pleasure Bound Book Six
Jan Springer

During a secret NASA mission to locate their brothers on the faraway planet of Paradise, the Hero sisters become separated after they crash land...and find unexpected romance with the tormented alien male warriors of the species in this ultra-long scifi book.

Taylor and Kayla

While searching for her brothers, Kayla Hero is bound and imprisoned by the Breeders— along with a male captive whose tantalizing scars pique her interest. Forced to escape with him, she's irresistibly aroused when she suddenly becomes *his* captive.

Wild lust flares in Kayla's eyes— a sensual side effect of the Fever Swamp water she's accidentally ingested. Taylor knows he will enjoy administering the cure — lots of sizzling hot lovemaking!

Blackie and Kinley

Injured and lost in a dense jungle, Kinley Hero is intimidated by the scarred man who hunts her, especially due to the power of erotic submission he holds over her.

Capturing his beautiful female prey, Blackie can't wait to train her as a pleasure slave for the Death Valley Boys. When her captor slips a collar around her neck, Kinley must struggle with lust as a natural submissive.

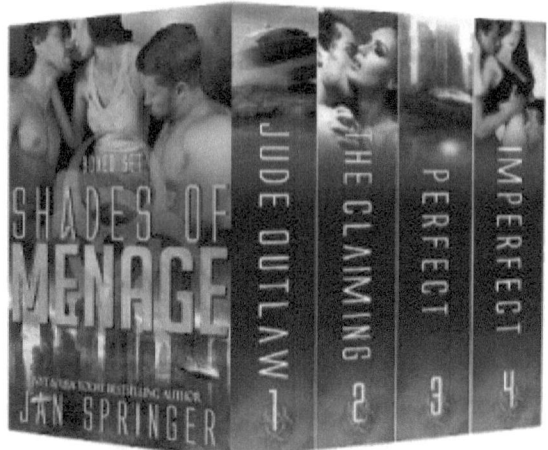

Shades of Ménage Boxed Set: Four Book Romance Ménage Collection

A fast-acting virus has killed a majority of the world's female population. Women's rights are stripped away and The Claiming Law is created, allowing groups of men to stake a claim on a female—as their sensual property.

After five years of fighting in the Terrorist Wars, the Outlaw brothers are coming home to declare ownership on the women they love...and they'll do it any way they can in **Jude Outlaw and The Claiming**.

PLUS

In the future...for population control, each human is embedded with a microchip that suppresses the urge to mate.

*Centuries later,...*A rebel group of young doctors are secretly tampering with their microchips and experimenting with intimacy. Now they search for allies who can help them with their cause – to eventually free humanity in the Dystopian Romance Ménage stories **"Perfect"** & **"Imperfect"**.

A CONTEMPORARY EROTIC ROMANCE BOXED SET
Naughty Girl Desires Boxed Set: Romance, Contemporary Romance, Romance Suspense, Box Set
(m/f only)

What You'll Find Inside Naughty Girl Desires
Jade's Fantasy
Kidnap Fantasies 1
Jan Springer

In the land of the rich and famous, Kidnap Fantasies is the answer to discreet naughty downtime.

When ex-downhill skier Jade Hart's two sisters give her a Kidnap Fantasies questionnaire, Jade is aroused at the prospect of having no-strings fun in the sun with a stranger whose only job would be to fulfill her every intimate fantasy. Although she knows she's too shy to send it in, she secretly pours her deepest wishes into the questionnaire.

Soon the questionnaire mysteriously vanishes and Jade's fantasy man appears on her luxury yacht in the form of a sexy handy man who gives her an intimate toy-filled Christmas holiday she'll never forget.

~*~

The Biker and The Bride
Jan Springer

Wrapped in red-hot lust for revenge, Avery plots to murder the man responsible for the death of her son. Her plans are dashed when her ex-husband crashes her wedding and whisks her away on his motorcycle to the rustic Canadian wilderness cabin they'd once honeymooned.

Police detective, Mason is fighting for Avery's love with everything he has.

Armed with whipped cream, handcuffs and his undying devotion, Mason vows he will make Avery love again. But it's only a matter of time before the man she'd planned to kill hunts them down...

~*~

Sinderella Sexy
Jan Springer

By day, she's a dedicated gynecologist.

By night, Dr. Ella Cinder, escapes reality by secretly performing in her own erotic, adult version of Cinderella, aptly re-titled Sinderella.

When sexy colleague Dr. Roarke Stephenson shows up in the Sinderella audience on the same night her Prince Charming stands her up, Ella seizes the opportunity to make Roarke into her Prince Charming for one carnal night of extremely naughty fun in front of an audience.

But at the strike of midnight, Ella knows she must face the harsh reality that Roarke must never learn her secret life and they can never be together again. Until then, she'll make sure he'll never forget their night of sensual play.

Dr. Roarke Stephenson is immediately captured by the lusciously curvy actress who hides behind a mask and is known only as Sinderella. For some insane reason she reminds him of his klutzy co-worker, Ella. But that's not possible. Ella would never have the nerve to do the wickedly delicious things Sinderella does to him, or would she?

~*~

Nice Girl Naughty
Jan Springer

Blind since nineteen, Summer has blossomed into a famous wood carver. When she's almost killed by a serial killer, she's whisked away to a secluded wilderness cabin by the man she once secretly loved. Summer can't get enough of touching professional bodyguard Nick Cassidy's thick, powerful muscles and all those other hard, yummy male body parts that she has always longed to explore.

For years Nick has stayed away from his best friend's kid sister, nice girl Summer. Now he's back, and sweeping his gorgeous redhead into the naughty cravings he's always had for her. With passion blinding him, Nick doesn't realize their hideout isn't safe—until it's too late.

Please note: The titles in Naughty Girl Desires have been previously published.

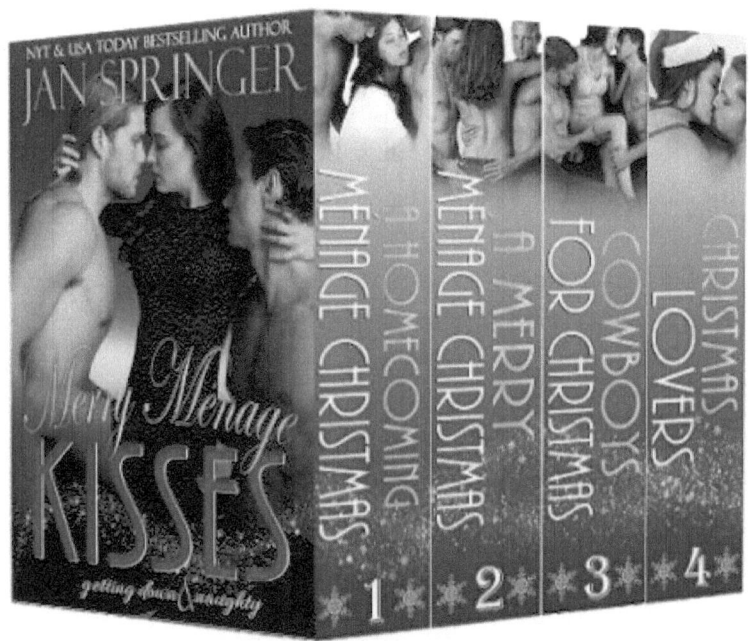

What You'll Find In The
Merry Ménage Kisses Boxed Set
Wrap yourself in four sexy holiday themed adult romance ménages.

A Homecoming Ménage Christmas

Jan Springer

Rachel has a *very* naughty secret and she's way too embarrassed to let anyone know about it. When The Key Club throws a Santa Fetish Ménage Night it's almost too good to be true. She *has* to figure out how to participate without anyone finding out!

Key Club bartenders Rob and Ron Simpson have fallen head over Santa hats for quiet, nice girl Rachel. But she has no clue how they feel about her. But she *will* know, because Rachel is coming home from a trip to Europe and the twin brothers are going to give her the best Homecoming Ménage Christmas ever. They'll do it with the help of some naughty toys, the Red Room, a safe word and...Santa Claus.

A Merry Ménage Christmas
Jan Springer

Dr. Kelsie Madison can't remember the last time she's had no-strings sex and that's her clue she's been working way too hard. It's time to unwind at the Key Club by indulging in a yummy Christmas present for herself. Something she's never experienced before - a red-hot ménage.

ER Dr. Ryder Greene and his roommate, physiotherapist, Dixon Flynn love sharing their women. They've had their eye on cute Dr. Kelsie Madison for quite some time, but she's a workaholic and she never has time to play.

When they learn she'll be at the Santa Claus Ménage Night festivities, they'll make sure they're the ones kissing Kelsie under the mistletoe.

And if they get their wish, Kelsie will be taking them home for Christmas.

Cowboys for Christmas
Jan Springer

Jennifer Jane (JJ) Watson has spent the past ten Christmases in a maximum-security prison.

The last thing she expects is to get early parole, along with a job on a remote Canadian cattle ranch serving Christmas holiday dinners to three of the sexiest cowboys she's ever met!

Rafe, Brady and Dan thought they were getting a couple of male ex-cons to help out around their secluded ranch, but instead they get an attractive and very appealing female.

In the snowbound wilds of Northern Ontario, female companionship is rare.

It's a good thing the three men like to share...

They're dominating, sexy-as-sin and they fill JJ with the hottest ménage fantasies she's ever had. Suddenly she's craving cowboys for Christmas and wishing for something she knows she can never have...a happily ever after.

Christmas Lovers
Jan Springer

Sergeant Connor Jordan, wounded overseas and sent back to the States to recuperate, just cannot stop fantasizing about the sexy nurse who cared for him. When his brothers give him a holiday gift certificate to Kidnap Fantasies, a top-secret fantasy organization, Connor knows he'll use their gift, if only to help him forget his wickedly delicious attraction to Nurse Sparks.

Nurse Tania Sparks has always been purely professional with her injured soldiers...until sinfully sexy Connor Jordan enters her hospital. He makes her body throb with an intense desire she's never known before. The last thing she wants is to get involved with the injured warrior. So what's a woman supposed to do to relieve her naughty frustrations? Call Kidnap Fantasies and have them supply her with a look-alike man who'll help her forget her sexy soldier...

When Tania and Connor unexpectedly come together at a secluded mountain chalet, their love explodes in a ménage of passion, sensuous desires and a happily forever after.

Contains ménage scenes.

For more Jan Springer stories, please visit
http://www.janspringer.com

_____

Jan's Newsletter

Hi! If you would like to get an email when my books are released, you can sign up here:

Newsletter: http://ymlp.com/xguembmugmgb

Your emails will never be shared and you can unsubscribe whenever you like.

Discover Other Titles by Jan Springer
http://www.janspringer.com

~*~

About the Author
Jan Springer writes full-time at her home nestled in cottage country, Ontario, Canada. She enjoys hiking, kayaking, gardening, reading and writing. She is a member of the Writers Union of Canada, Romance Writers of America. She loves hearing from her readers.

A Word From The Author
Hi! Thank you for purchasing this book. Word of mouth is important for any author to succeed. If you enjoyed this story feel free to leave a short review at the place where you bought it. I would really appreciate it. I look forward to bringing you more stories in the near future. Thanks!

If you would like to contact me or personally send me feedback, you can reach me by using my contact page at: http://janspringerauthor.wordpress.com/contact/

Here are other ways we can connect:
Jan Springer Website at http://www.janspringer.com
Facebook - https://www.facebook.com/janspringereroticromance
Twitter - https://twitter.com/janspringer @janspringer
Pinterest - http://www.pinterest.com/janspringer1/
Jan's Blog - http://janspringerauthor.wordpress.com/blog-2/
LinkedIn - http://ca.linkedin.com/in/janspringerauthor/
Google Plus - https://plus.google.com/u/0/
101527334949931513035/posts
Jan's Newsletter - http://ymlp.com/xguembmugmgb
Goodreads - https://www.goodreads.com/author/show/
260628.Jan_Springer
Happy Reading,
jan springer

Don't miss out!

Visit the website below and you can sign up to receive emails whenever Jan Springer publishes a new book. There's no charge and no obligation.

https://books2read.com/r/B-A-WGQ-QJMF

BOOKS 2 READ

Connecting independent readers to independent writers.